YA
2016

W9-ACS-750

DISCARD

WEST GEORGIA REGIONAL LIBRARY SYSTEM

Come Next Spring

Come Next Spring

ALANA WHITE

Clarion Books

New York

Clarion Books
a Houghton Mifflin Company imprint
215 Park Avenue South, New York, NY 10003
Text copyright © 1990 by Alana J. White

All rights reserved.
For information about permission to reproduce
selections from this book, write to Permissions,
Houghton Mifflin Company, 2 Park Street, Boston, MA 02108.
Printed in the USA

Library of Congress Cataloging-in-Publication Data

White, Alana J.
  Come next spring / Alana J. White.
    p. cm.
  Summary: In 1949, in the Smoky Mountains of Tennessee, Salina
struggles to accept the inevitability of change—a highway cutting
through farmland, a brother and sister starting their own lives, and
nothing left in common with her best friend.
  ISBN 0-395-52593-4
  [1. Change—Fiction. 2. Mountain life—Fiction. 3. Great Smoky
Mountains (N.C. and Tenn.)—Fiction.] 1. Title.
PZ7.W5817Co 1990
[Fic]—dc20   89-37156
                          CIP
                          AC

BP 10 9 8 7 6 5 4 3 2 1

To my parents, Jane and Fred Thomas

426681   WEST GEORGIA REGIONAL LIBRARY SYSTEM

In 1949, spring came early to Tennessee. In mid-February, before the last of the winter storms, pinkish-white mayflowers began carpeting the evergreen and oak woodlands, filling the air with a spicy fragrance. As the cold, quiet months of winter slowly gave way to the March sun, the earth warmed and the leaves on the trees covering the Great Smoky Mountains turned dark blue-green. Down in Pine Valley, Salina Harris watched the tulips in her mother's flower garden push through the ground and open scarlet petals to the sun, and in April she celebrated her twelfth birthday not once, but twice: in her seventh-grade class, horsing around with the other kids in her room and being a nuisance to Miss Williams, and at home, after supper, with her family pressing around the kitchen table, singing loudly off-key as she leaned forward and blew out the candles on a Tennessee jam cake.

And then suddenly it was summer, and she was out of school. In June, the laurel that had bloomed in late spring at low elevations spread upward on the moun-

tains, covering them in pink and white blossoms. Salina helped her mother and Mary hang the wash on the clothesline in the back yard, Salina talking a blue streak. And in the evenings, she and Mark prisoned lightning bugs in a Mason jar and stabbed holes in the lid so that the bugs could breathe. Sometimes at night she and Mark and Paul would make a train, holding on to each others' waists and zigzagging around the trees in the front yard. Paul was always the engine, Salina was always in the middle, and Mark was always the caboose. Salina thoroughly enjoyed those evenings with her brothers, for far too often lately Paul was in the barn, hovering over Sugar-Boy, his sickly colt, or trooping off with the other boys, instead of stirring up some commotion with her, like he used to do.

At Minnie Myrtle Wilson's Dry Goods Store, Salina bought a box of rose-scented stationery with a big red S at the top of the pages and wrote clever letters to her best pal, Mayella Crenshaw, who was in Sevierville for the summer. She made tomato catsup which no one would touch, and she canned and quilted. She tended the pigs—a job she hated—and ate huge bowls of her daddy's homemade banana ice cream. She visited the bookmobile on Saturdays, and she wrote two stories, and she loved Gone With the Wind so much, she read it twice. From June through August, time unwound in a smooth straight line, and each day was the same or a variation of that sameness. Those ordinary days Salina embraced, and she expected life to go on that way forever.

✥ ONE ✥

O N THE FIRST DAY of school, Salina woke early
and could not go back to sleep. The September
sky outside her bedroom window was sunny with
pink clouds drifting across it. In the distance lay the
Smoky Mountains, blanketed in blue-gray mist.

Salina's mind raced ahead into the morning. In a
while, she and Mary would get up and go downstairs, and after a big breakfast, she and Paul—and
this year, Mark—would walk to Pine Valley School
together, three Harris kids strung across Sand Lick
Road. And finally, in her classroom at last, she
would once again see Mayella.

"Mary," she whispered when she couldn't stand
waiting a minute longer. "Come on. Wake up!"

She nudged her sister in the ribs, then hopped
from bed and hurried to the dresser. The floor was
bare, and this morning the wooden planks felt cold
to her naked feet. After slipping on her dress and
splashing her face with water from the porcelain

basin, she studied her reflection in the mirror. There she stood, a tall, skinny eighth-grader with unruly red hair.

"Yipes," she muttered, mashing her hair down around her head. It sprang back up the moment she released it. She glanced at the black and white magazine photo of Clark Gable stuck along the frame's edge and took another look at herself.

The freckles splotching her nose and cheeks looked as big and brown as always; bigger, maybe, because of the summer sun and all those afternoons swimming in Abrams Creek. Once, she had tried bleaching her freckles with lemons, like Mayella suggested. It hadn't worked.

"Yipes," she muttered again—and glancing across the room to the feather bed, saw that Mary had not moved one inch. "Mary," she said, as she worked the brush through her hair, "come on, now, it's getting late."

Mary lay still and gazed back at her, dreamy-eyed and content, before slowly unwinding herself from the tangled sheets. Mary was nineteen, a graduate of Pine Valley High School, and since Christmas she had been engaged to Hank White. Hank had joined the military service in June and was stationed in Texas. Mary would see him in December, when he came home on furlough. With the engagement had come a certain laziness, and though something about Mary's self-satisfied new look intrigued Salina, the overall change irritated her. She watched

[4]

impatiently while her sister stood before the dresser and ran a comb through her hair—shiny brown hair that always fluffed and curled at the ends in a perfect way.

"Just look at *you*," Mary said. "I swear I've never seen anybody so antsy about the first day of school."

Salina smiled. "I'm not antsy. I'm looking forward to seeing Mayella, that's all."

"She back?"

"Yep. Mr. Crenshaw was bringing her and her mom home from Sevierville last night."

Mary eased the lid off the round cardboard box on her cosmetics tray and leisurely powdered her arms and neck. "Wish I had a rich Aunt Lucy to spend the summer with."

"Not me—I'll take Pine Valley over Sevierville any day of the week." Salina glanced toward the bedroom door.

Mary gave no notice.

"I smell ham frying. Breakfast must be about ready."

Mary said nothing.

"Everybody's waiting for us."

Mary touched her index finger to the tip of her tongue and ran her dampened finger over one light brown eyebow, and then the other. "You go on," she murmured. "I'll be down later."

"Later?" Salina's brown eyes widened. "But you never miss breakfast!" She folded her arms across her chest and gazed at her sister. "I'll just wait."

Mary concentrated on her reflection. "I got my period in the middle of the night. You go on. Tell Mama for me."

"But *Mary*," Salina wheedled.

Mary scowled at Salina in the mirror and said in a complaining voice, "For Pete's sake, what difference does it make? I don't feel good and I'm not hungry! Anyway, I want to lose five pounds before Christmas." She leaned over the dresser, closer to the glass to inspect one side of her nose. "And *stop* gawking at me."

"Well, good grief," Salina said. She watched Mary a moment longer before heading downstairs and into the kitchen.

Watery sunlight filtered through the windows, giving the room a vague blue light. As always, the oak table was set for breakfast, but Paul, Mark, her daddy—this morning their chairs were vacant.

Salina drew her brow into a light frown and regarded her mother steadily. "Just exactly where is everybody?"

Anna Harris removed a pan of crusty biscuits from the oven. "Good morning," she said pleasantly.

Salina bit her lip. "Good morning."

"They're in the barn. Supposed to be checking over the tractor." Her mother's brown eyes were teasing. "They're watching Sugar-Boy, I imagine."

Salina walked farther into the kitchen, giving herself a view of the barn. "That figures. They're always watching that horse, especially Paul."

Her brother had come by Sugar-Boy in a curious way. The foal was premature and at church his owner, Homer Joiner, said he was too old to fool with keeping the sickly thing alive. Since old Doc Sharp's passing, people tended their ailing livestock themselves. If they really needed help, they prayed for the traveling vet to come around. Finally, Paul had stepped in—he'd buy the foal, he said. And he had paid Homer Joiner ten dollars.

For the next few weeks, Paul had practically moved into the barn with the foal, keeping an eye on him, dipping a damp cloth in sugar-water for him to suck. Sugar had lived and become the center of Paul's life, and lately it seemed to Salina her brother didn't take much time for anyone else . . . not even her, anymore. They had always been such pals, exploring mountain trails, playing on the same team at school . . . till he transferred to the high school building. Not that she didn't love Mark and Mary; she did. But Mark was young, and Mary never seemed to have fun.

"I wish Homer Joiner hadn't sold Paul that horse," Salina said now. To her mind, the only spark of interest Sugar had ever caused had occurred a couple of months ago in mid-June, when Michael Burmeister appeared at the farm in his truck, hoping to drum up some business. Burmeister was new in town, a veterinarian, and so far he had not gotten much work in Pine Valley.

Besides being a stranger to the community, the

young newcomer was German. An outlander if ever there was one, since not long ago America had fought a war against the Germans.

That afternoon John Harris had treated Burmeister cordially, saying things were fine these days and mentioning Sugar's close call.

"Why don't I take a quick look at him?" said the young man, who was tall, slender, and fair.

"No need," answered Paul, moving slightly to block the man's way to the barn.

When Michael Burmeister left, Paul had shaken his hand, but his face had remained grim.

"Where's Mary?" Anna Harris said. She stirred the grits bubbling in a cast-iron pot on the stove.

"She's coming. She doesn't feel good."

"It's certainly not like her to miss breakfast."

Salina cast her mother a sly look. "She's on a diet."

"A diet? Mary? Why, she's already skinny! It didn't look to me like she was on a diet at the picnic yesterday, eating all Miss Minnie's pecan pie."

Salina ran her finger along the cabinet of the black sewing machine that had been Old Mama's. "'I want to lose five pounds before Christmas.' That is exactly what she said."

Salina's mother laughed softly. "I knew it: love."

"Then I am never going to be in love," vowed Salina. "Not ever. I'm not ever letting it get *me* crazy."

"Never say never, Salina. Are you looking forward to seeing Mayella at school today? The Crenshaws must have gotten home awfully late last night to have missed the Labor Day picnic."

"I sure am." Salina's face brightened.

"I know you two will have a good time."

Salina nodded, true, and glanced at the clock over the refrigerator. "We will if I ever get to school. Guess I'll just have to go after Daddy and those two brothers of mine. The darn ham will be cold as ice."

After the bright morning, the inside of the barn looked black to Salina's eyes. She stood in the doorway and squinted to make out her father and brothers. "Daddy?"

"Come on in, Salina," he called softly.

Paul shushed her and Mark held a warning finger to his lips as Salina stepped over the threshold into the stillness of the barn. "Be real quiet," Paul said. "Sugar's sound asleep."

She peered into the stall where the horse lay sleeping. He was going on eleven months, and she did not understand the fuss. He was small for his age, but doing well. Still, she kept her voice low. "Y'all come on. Mama's got breakfast ready."

"Good," Paul grinned. "I'm starving."

"You're always starving."

"I'm a growing boy."

Paul was the image of their father, dark-skinned, with eyes and hair that were almost black. His hair was slightly long. He was a good-looking boy, people around Sevier County said so, especially the women at the Hogginsville Free Will Baptist Church. Make a fine man when he got his knots worked out. Right now, as far as Salina was concerned, Paul had a stubborn streak as wide as Pine Valley.

Take two weeks ago: Paul had shirked his chores to go fishing with his pals, though John Harris had warned him not to leave till his work around the farm was done. Naturally, he got caught and wasn't allowed to go anywhere except to church for a week. "What difference does it make when I finish painting the fence as long as it gets done?" he'd said to his dad.

"Your mother and I set the schedules around here," John Harris had reminded him. "Not you."

Today, Paul was beginning his senior year at Pine Valley High School: an official member of the graduating class of 1950.

"Me, too," Mark piped. "I'm starving, too."

"Then come on. I don't want us tardy the first day."

Paul shook his head. "I'm not gonna be tardy. I'm not going, period."

Salina stared at him. "Not going?" she said, "what do you mean, you're not going?" and her voice was too loud for the barn.

Paul nodded toward Sugar-Boy. "Hush. You'll wake him. Come on. Mama'll be out here after us in a minute."

"She should be," John Harris said. "No excuse in us not being ready for breakfast." He removed his straw hat from a rusty nail in the wall and started for the barn door, limping slightly. No matter how much his leg ached, he never complained. "Least I can feel it," he always said.

Going across the back yard, Salina lengthened her stride to match Paul's. He had on his black and red flannel shirt and his faded denim jacket and brand-new Levi jeans and new boots. He was right. He was a growing boy. Suddenly, he towered over her.

"I'm going to Sevierville with Daddy to help pick out new parts for the tractor," he said boastfully.

"*Sevierville?* How come everybody's going to Sevierville all of a sudden?"

"After–Labor Day sale starts at noon today," Salina's daddy explained.

She touched Paul's elbow. "But you're a senior, and this is the first day of school. You can't just lay out—"

"Slow down!" Mark cried. He grabbed Salina's hand and stumbled along with her, his short legs struggling to match her pace. "*I'm* going to school today. *I'm* still here."

Paul turned his dark eyes on Salina and shook back his hair. "I'm not laying out. Daddy talked to Mr. Green about it and got special permission." Sam Green was the principal of Pine Valley School.

[11]

"Daddy told Mr. Green he needs my help."

"But—"

"But what?"

She trailed after him, onto the screened-in back porch and into the kitchen. "I thought we'd be walking to school together today, like always. Like we always used to do."

"You're nuts," Paul said.

They sat at the kitchen table and ate scrambled eggs and ham, biscuits and grits and homemade pear preserves, everybody talking but Salina. Mary's chair was vacant. "Tell you one thing I'm gonna do in Sevierville," Paul declared at one point. "I'm gonna check around and see if people have heard anything about the surveyors Homer mentioned."

One Saturday morning in July, Homer Joiner had been complaining about a team of surveyors he claimed he had seen nosing around Sand Lick Road.

"Fine," John Harris answered. "If we have time." He took a look at Salina and added, "Wow, how about that new dress you've got on. Did you make that, or your mama?"

"Mama," Salina said, though she did not much want to talk. "She copied it out of the Monkey Ward catalogue."

"Well, it's a peach! I sure do like those little yellow flowers on it. Want some more milk?"

"No, Sir."

"Better have some, you've got to keep good and

strong if you're going to be smartest in the class again this year."

Salina wondered what in the world being strong had to do with being smart, but she kept her mouth shut and poured herself a half glass of milk from the china pitcher.

"I sewed on the buttons," Mark whispered, and Paul snickered.

Salina kept still. She felt sour, although she couldn't say why. Who cared if Mary stayed upstairs? Let her stay in the bedroom and rot if she wanted. And who cared if Paul Harris wasn't going to school today? Certainly not her. It would be crazy to care one iota about that. Skipping school together—that was something else they used to do.

"All the way down the front," Mark said.

Paul rested his elbow on the top of Mark's head and gazed at Salina innocently. "How come a six-year-old can sew on buttons better than you?"

Mark watched and listened quietly.

"Because she's suddenly developed a severe case of butterfingers," John Harris said with a smile.

Salina put down her fork. It was true. These days anything she touched broke into a thousand pieces. "I don't know why," she answered.

"Am I smart now?" Mark asked.

Salina narrowed her eyes critically. "What was that?"

"Today I'm in first grade. So am I smart now?"

Salina stared at Mark, at the bright red hair, the chubby arms, the brownish-orange freckles on his cheeks. They looked just like hers.

"You're as stupid as ever," she informed him.

"Salina!" her daddy said sharply.

She studied her plate, her face flaming. "Yes, Sir," she said, and for good measure, she added, "I'm sorry, Mark," though she felt mean and stubborn and was not sorry at all.

After breakfast, she and Mark left the house together and walked down Sand Lick Road. Spotting some goldenrod, Salina plucked a blossom and stuck the stem in her mouth.

Mark said softly, "I'm getting a punkin."

"*Pumpkin?*" Salina answered, and with one flick of her finger sent the stem sailing through the air. "What're you talking about, ding-bat?"

"On Halloween night, I'm going to get a big orange punkin and carve a funny face in it and wear it over my head. Nobody will know me. And later, I'll make some punkin pies."

Salina groaned. "I have heard some crazy, ignorant ideas, Mark Harris, but that one is the craziest! That one takes the fruitcake. In the first place, where would you get a pumpkin big enough to wear over your head?"

"Punkin Junction," he said. "Or maybe Miss Minnie's."

Salina closed her ears to him. In the distance lay the mountains. To Salina, fall was the prettiest

[14]

season in the Smokies. Unfortunately, that was when tourists crossed the mountain road by the thousands.

"Honestly," Mark said, pulling her sleeve, "don't you think I should have gone to Sevierville with Daddy and Paul today?"

"No," she answered. "You can't miss school." To her surprise, they had already passed Mayella's rich house and Miss Minnie's dilapidated store with the rusty gas pump out front.

"Paul's missing school. First day."

"Doesn't matter," she continued. "He's older."

The school buildings came into view, and both the high school and elementary school bells rang.

They walked down the hallway, their footsteps echoing around them, Salina yanking Mark's wrist. "Look here. Everybody else is in class. You better get settled quick, Mark Harris, because darn if I like being late because of you! I *was* planning to talk to Mayella Crenshaw before the bell rang, but *huh*-uh."

When they reached the doorway to Ida Carson's first grade, Mark pulled away from Salina. "You just go on then. I'm not scared." Without another word, he took a desk, slid his lunch pail in the space beneath his seat and turned to Mandy Phelps, his best friend.

Salina stood in the doorway feeling like a big no-good. She remembered clearly how scared she was on her first day of school, even though Paul had walked her to her room. "Mark," she called softly, but he did not respond. He and Mandy were watching Jimmy Don Orange and laughing behind their hands.

Six little kids in the first-grade class, and Jimmy Don the only one accompanied by an adult—his grandmother, Mrs. Imy June Orange, who apparently did not care that all the kids had pre-registered. The silver-haired woman stood bent over Jimmy Don, straightening his wide, white collar. His hair was slicked against his head.

Salina looked at Mark. The morning sun slanted through the windows, touching his silky red hair, making the freckles stand out on his cheeks and arms. Suddenly a memory bloomed in Salina's inner eye: her mother meeting her and Mary and Paul on Sand Lick Road on sunny afternoons, walking the rest of the way home from school with them, Mark, a baby, sitting in his red wagon, being pulled behind, chattering to himself. And now Mark was in first grade, and she was in the eighth, and next year—why, she would be in the high school building, and Paul would be a graduate, and Mary might even be married. And then what? What then? A funny, new feeling took hold of Salina, and for one brief moment, she was afraid, her stomach curling in on itself.

"Mark," she called, urgent this time, and he turned. "You be good and this afternoon I'll meet you out front on the steps. Okay?"

"Okay," he replied, his expression sweet.

≈§ *TWO* §≈

*T*HE WOODEN FLOOR squeaked beneath Salina's feet.

"Salina," Miss Williams said. "I wondered where you were." Rebecca Williams's chestnut hair was pulled into a bun at the nape of her neck. Though in her mid-twenties, she was still single and lived with her father in Hogginsville.

Salina smiled cheerfully. "Yes, Ma'am, I'm sorry I'm late. I accompanied Mark to class. It's his first day." She looked at Mayella, happy at last. Mayella grinned and shook back her curly black hair.

"I was just reviewing our daily schedule. Go ahead and be seated."

"Just wait till lunch! I have a *zillion* things to tell you," Mayella whispered loudly as Salina took the desk beside her. Johnny Campbell made a face, and Frank Talley yanked Salina's hair.

Salina smacked Frank's hand and said "Hey" to

Abigail Cooper. Mayella Crenshaw was still the prettiest girl in class. Abigail, who was chubby and wore her long hair in Shirley Temple curls, had on the new glasses she and her mom had picked out in Pigeon Forge. Next to Mayella, Abigail was Salina's best friend.

"We have a new student," announced Miss Williams. "Though I'm sure some of you know Scooter Russell from church."

Everyone promptly turned and stared at the white-haired girl who had taken a seat in the back corner away from the windows, near the wood-burning stove. Despite the big smile on her face, she turned pink. Though Salina had noticed Scooter Russell in church, she didn't know much about her. She remembered Scooter's father vaguely, since he had been from the valley. Scooter's mother was from Maryville. Lena Russell and her five girls had moved to the valley a few weeks ago.

"Scooter," said Miss Williams, "stand up so everyone can see you."

Scooter did as bidden. She was small for twelve, her hair snow white. Johnny Campbell whistled appreciatively, and the pink in the new girl's cheeks deepened to a scarlet hue.

"That's uncalled for," Miss Williams informed the boy.

"*I'll* say," Mayella commented to Salina, who snickered. She couldn't imagine anyone ever whistling at Scooter Russell and meaning it.

"Scooter sings and plays the banjo," Miss Williams informed the students. "Don't you, Scooter?" The white-haired girl nodded silently, her smile tacked in place. "So we'll have some music at lunchtime today, won't that be fun?"

No one answered, and Scooter sat down.

Salina glanced at Abigail. "Sure am glad *I'm* not new." She slumped comfortably into her desk.

"Class," Miss Williams went on, "this year I'm having everyone do a special project." Everyone groaned. "It'll be fun. You'll each have a partner, and the assignments won't be due until the Monday after Thanksgiving."

Mayella caught Salina's eye. "Me and you," she mouthed.

Salina nodded happily. This year was going to be great—better than seventh grade, even.

"I'll assign topics and partners early next week. And by the way, on Friday, we're taking a field trip to the Sugarlands."

Salina straightened in the desk; field trips were rare. "The Sugarlands is almost ten miles away."

"That's right," agreed Miss Williams. "Sugarland Mountain is inside the park boundary."

Also within the Smoky Mountain National Park were Laurel Falls and Cove Mountain and, farther off, Cherokee Orchard. Salina had never traveled to any of those places; there were ample streams to wade in and wooded trails to explore outside the park, in Pine Valley. In the old days, before the U.S. government forced them out, mountain people lived in the remote gorges of the Sugarlands. The area was called "Moonshiners' Paradise" and "Blockaders' Glory."

A shiver of excitement ran down Salina's spine. "Neat."

At noon the school bell rang for lunch and within a few minutes the eighth-grade boys had eaten and were on the high school field playing kickball. The girls and Miss Williams settled beneath the ancient maple in the side yard.

"Scooter," Miss Williams said, "why don't you play something for us?"

"Okay." The new girl started tuning her battered old banjo.

"Wait'll you hear about my cousin Jim!" Mayella blurted to the circle of girls. "He's the cutest boy you've ever seen!"

"You got a picture?" Jolene Henderson asked.

"Uh-huh, right here!"

"Girls," Miss Williams said, "Scooter's about ready."

"Give it, give it!" Abigail snatched the photo and pushed her new glasses back on the bridge of her nose. "Wow!"

"He's a senior and he plays senior basketball and he's the team captain," Mayella told them proudly.

Salina scrutinized the black-and-white photo Abby handed her. Jim Johnson might be okay, but he was not handsome like Paul. She didn't see much to get excited about. "He is as cute as pie," she said.

"Uh-huh," Mayella agreed, her green eyes flashing, "and when we have our taffy pull on Halloween, everybody can see him, because this year he and my aunt are coming all the way from Sevierville!"

"Here goes," Scooter said, and began softly singing and playing an upbeat tune.

"Oh, *brother*," Mayella grumbled in a soft voice to Salina. "For somebody as hard up and homely as she is, that girl seems mighty happy."

Salina tucked the hem of her dress around her bare legs. Since the war, she had been told, Scooter had no daddy. No daddy, and four sisters, and every night since moving to Pine Valley from Signal Mountain, her mother had worked in the fields until dark with her girls. Salina did not want to think about somebody's father being killed in a place none of them had ever heard of, and she especially did not want to think about how the same thing might have happened to her own daddy, but for the tractor accident that had permanently injured his leg and kept him home from the war.

So she considered instead how crazy it was that in spite of everything, Scooter Russell seemed content. That did not strike Salina as right. What kind of girl was Scooter Russell, anyway? What kind of person was any girl who could get over something as terrible as that? Scooter's eyes did not look the least bit sad.

One thing for certain, though: Scooter sure could pick the banjo. Salina loved music and couldn't help tapping her foot in time with Scooter's song.

That afternoon at two o'clock Miss Williams said, "Class, I have a surprise."

Salina's library book was on the floor, beneath her desk. She froze, bent over sideways, her fingers touching its cover. She didn't want a surprise. This was the time of day when in seventh grade she could count on Miss Williams giving them free time to begin their lessons, and to Salina that was the best time of the entire school day. That was when she could read for a while, books like *Jane Eyre*, or *The Man in the Iron Mask*, or *The Three Musketeers*—any of the novels she might have checked from the bookmobile the previous Saturday.

Miss Williams did not mind that she sneaked around and read instead of studied. On Fridays when they had the new *Junior Scholastic* magazine in their hands, Salina would prop hers up in a clever way to hide her library book, and Miss Williams would not call on her. She would go down the rows asking questions and slide her gray eyes over Salina Harris. It was an unspoken, secret understanding between them.

"Since it's the first day of school," Miss Williams said, "I'm going to let each of you tell how you spent your summer."

"Let?" Salina said. "Everybody in Pine Valley always knows exactly what everyone else is doing." And anyway, she wanted to read.

Mayella's hand shot into the air: "Me!" she cried. "Me first, pleaaase, Miss Williams!"

But Miss Williams said, "Why don't we have someone else go first," and surveyed the classroom for targets.

Salina slipped down in her seat.

"Scooter?" Rebecca Williams said.

Scooter Russell walked to the front of the room. "We got ready to move to Pine Valley. And when we arrived in August, we sold seven quilts we had made. We took them straight to Minnie Myrtle Wilson's Dry Goods, and last week she sold them to the tourist shops in Gatlinburg."

Salina raised her brow. "Selling crafts to the tourists invading the mountains is not something I personally would brag about," she said.

Miss Williams gave her a warning look.

"I wasn't bragging. We needed the money, that's all." Scooter sat back down, and again Miss Williams searched the room.

Mayella waved her hand vigorously.

"Abigail?" the teacher said.

Mayella sulked, Abigail told about her trip to Pigeon Forge, and Willard Tucker bragged about the eight-foot snake his father had killed in the Tuckers' kitchen.

When Willard returned to his seat, the back of Salina's neck prickled.

"Salina?" Miss Williams said. "We haven't heard from you."

Salina stood at the head of the class and could not think of one exciting thing to tell about her summer.

After a moment her teacher said, "Well—what did you do?"

"Nothing special," Salina answered. In a cheery voice she added, "Just the same old stuff, but I had a real good time."

"Oh? Did you keep a journal like I suggested?"

Salina stared at the floor. She had hoped her teacher would forget about that. "No, Ma'am," she answered quietly.

"Any writing? Surely you wrote some stories."

Salina didn't like anyone mentioning the stories she wrote. It embarrassed her. "Two," she said, squeezing her toes in the tips of her black and white saddle oxfords. "I wrote two."

"That's *wonderful*," Miss Williams exclaimed. "Perhaps sometime you'll read them for us?"

Panic beat in Salina's throat. Never, she thought. She did not write like a real person. She did not know how to put down the first sentence, and when she finally did get one, none of the others would come into her head for a long, long time. It was like the story was floating in space somewhere and all she had to do was think of it, but she never had much luck. She didn't think she would write any more stories; it was too hard and made her hurt inside to be so stupid with a foggy brain. She could tell she was not a real writer, because writing was not easy for her like it was for Sir Walter Scott and Charlotte Brontë and for Margaret Mitchell, who had written *Gone With the Wind*.

"*Gone With the Wind*," Salina said. "I read *Gone With the Wind*, twice."

Mayella squirmed in her seat and waved her hand.

"I think in the dozen or so years since that book was published, everyone in the nation has read it," Miss Williams said. "Mayella?"

Mayella rushed to the front of the room. "I had the best summer of anybody," she announced, "because guess what?" Without giving anyone a chance to guess anything, she finished, "I SAW *Gone With the Wind*!!!"

Salina gasped. "A picture show?" She—in fact, few of them, if any—had ever seen a movie. "With Clark Gable and Vivien Leigh?"

"Uh-huh, and it was just wonderful, and I saw three more movies, one called *A Date with Judy*, starring Elizabeth Taylor and Jane Powell, and one—"

"Mayella," Miss Williams said, "that's nice, but will you tell the class about the theater and all?"

"It was huge and black inside where the screen is, but in the lobby it's like a circus. They sell popcorn and candy and gum, and there was this *beautiful* big poster of Rhett and Scarlett with the city of Atlanta on fire in the background."

Salina heard little of this. She was thinking about seeing a picture show. She was thinking about watching Clark Gable and Vivien Leigh make a book come true. And Clark Gable! Why, he was her very favorite movie star. She thought of the photograph on her dresser mirror, carefully torn from the pages of one of the *Photoplay* magazines Mayella's Aunt Lucy forwarded to Mayella. In it, Clark Gable was smiling sadly. But it wasn't the smile that touched Salina's heart. It was the expression in his eyes, like he knew a heartbreaking secret.

"How would you say the movie compares to the novel," Miss Williams prompted. "I mean, as far as the plot goes?"

Mayella wrinkled her nose disdainfully. "I haven't read the book—but the movie's just *wonderful* and so sad at the end when Captain Butler leaves Scarlett. The best part's at the *very* last, when Scarlett sinks down on the stairway. She knows he'll be back. 'Tomorrow is another day,'" Mayella quoted dreamily, her hand covering her heart, "and, oh, it is so romantic!"

"But he's not *coming* back," Scooter Russell announced from her corner in the back of the schoolroom.

Salina twisted around and stared at the girl. "What do you *mean,* he's not coming back?"

"He said he wasn't. I don't know how it could've been much clearer, it was right there in black and white on the page: 'My dear, I don't give a damn.'"

Salina's cheeks flamed. "You're crazy—"

"Salina," Miss Williams said. "Watch your temper."

"—Rhett Butler loved Scarlett O'Hara," Salina stated. "He came back to her, and everybody knows it. He *had* to."

"Why do you say that?" prompted Miss Williams.

Mayella folded her arms impatiently over her chest, still standing in front of the class. "Can't I just tell some more about my summer? My Aunt Lucy bought me a baton and some white majorette boots—"

But Miss Williams was looking at Salina.

"Because," Salina answered firmly, "otherwise, it's all too sad. Not to mention unfair. He had to come back to make everything work out right in the end." She regarded Scooter. "How did you come up with such a screwball idea?"

Mayella returned to the desk beside Salina and plopped down in it.

In the face of Scooter's silence, Salina asked confidently, "What do you think, Miss Williams?"

The young woman hesitated. "I think that the question of whether or not Captain Butler might return to Scarlett, giving us a romantic ending, is left open; that is, maybe he does and maybe he doesn't. I think it simply depends on how you feel about things. And I'm not at all sure fairness has anything to do with it. Now, I'd better put your homework assignment on the board—"

Salina sat still. She felt betrayed. How could Rebecca Williams be so wrong? She had thought Miss Williams knew everything. She looked toward the back corner of the room, directly into Scooter Russell's content little face.

"He . . . came . . . *back*," Salina said, mouthing each word with great care, making certain the white-haired girl got every single syllable. Then she looked at Mayella and grinned.

⋖ *THREE* ⋗

Aᴺᴺᴬ Hᴀʀʀɪꜱ ꜱʟɪᴅ the blackberry pies into the oven before turning her attention to Mark. "What about recess? What did Mrs. Carson have you do then?"

He crumbled a hunk of cold cornbread in a tall glass of homemade buttermilk and mixed the concoction with a tablespoon. "We played Blindman's Bluff and Red Rover."

"Good grief," Salina said, and locked her feet firmly around the front legs of her chair. Mary was at the sink, finishing the dishes. Salina frowned, her mouth puckered. Usually at this time of day, Mary was upstairs mooning and writing love letters to Hank, and Mark and Paul were in the barn. Those were the good times with her mother—when they were alone, and she could talk without an audience. "Mark," she said, "why don't you just go on outside and play some more?"

"Don't want to," he answered, "'less you play, too."

"I'm not playing any silly kid games."

Mary snickered. "Since when?"

Salina threw her sister a dirty look. She wished Mary would get out of her sight. For someone who was so sick she couldn't come downstairs this morning, she sure looked chipper now.

"You always did *before*," Mark said accusingly to Salina, but before what, he did not say. He took a drink from the glass, swiped at his milk mustache with his free hand and started for the screened-in porch. "Sugar-Boy missed me today. I just bet he did."

"Be careful with that glass," his mother called after him.

"Mama," Salina said the minute the screen door slammed behind Mark, "guess what!"

Her mother finished wiping the counter top. "What?"

"You know Mayella spent the summer in Sevierville? While she was there, she went to the movies a hundred times, and she saw *Gone With the Wind*!"

Mary turned from the sink, excitement shining in her hazel eyes. "With Clark Gable and Vivien Leigh?"

"No," retorted Salina, "with Peter Pan and Tinkerbell."

"Oh!" Mary hissed. "Sometimes, Salina Harris!"

Salina poked out her chin. "Sometimes what?"

Mary planted her hands firmly on her hips and bent forward a bit at the waist. *"Sometimes, I just don't know!"* She looked at their mother. "I'm going upstairs to write some letters."

For a time neither Salina nor her mother spoke. Anna Harris dried the tin measuring cup and put it in the cabinet while Salina gazed out the windows, wondering exactly when she had turned bad. Slowly the silence of the kitchen mashed in on her, and when she could not tolerate it a moment longer, she said, "Do you know the Russells?"

Her mother relaxed against the counter. "Certainly."

"Well, Scooter Russell's in eighth grade, and she's a case." Her mother made no comment. "She's *puny*," Salina complained. "And her dumb hair's solid white."

In the distance, dust rose on Sand Lick Road. "Here comes your father. Salina, Scooter may be small for her age, but she's a pretty girl. And she has a lovely singing voice."

Salina clicked her tongue in disgust, thinking, So what?

"Her family has certainly had a hard time. I doubt Lena would have moved in with Granny Russell if she could have supported herself and the girls after Scooter's father died. It's a good thing Howard's helping them out around the place."

Howard Gardner, a tall, lanky redhead with a warm smile for everyone—especially Sally Russell, who was Scooter's sister and Mary's age. In fact, Salina had heard all about Sally and Howard from Mary, who had immediately befriended Sally. Sally moved to Pine Valley with her mother and sisters, and love grabbed hold of Howard Gardner. Salina didn't blame Howard for admiring Sally. She had honey-blond hair and clear blue eyes that almost sparkled as she and her sisters sang in the church choir on Sunday morning.

Salina frowned suddenly. She didn't want to think about Sally and Howard, or about Scooter Russell being a pretty girl, or about how well Scooter sang. She wanted to think about her being dead wrong about Rhett Butler.

Pushing back from the table, she went to the screen door and watched the green pickup truck move slowly along the drive and stop at the barn; watched her daddy climb from the front seat, then Paul, who angrily slammed his door shut. What's he so mad about, Salina wondered.

For a time, Paul and her father stood talking beside the truck, then her daddy slung his arm around Paul's shoulders, and they rounded the barn and disappeared from view.

Salina started outside.

"Salina," her mother said after her, "you stay here and set the table while I make biscuits for supper."

"I'll be right back," she promised, "but Mayella invited me to her house for supper tonight. I told her it would be okay."

"Salina, don't start this. You're not supposed to go out on school nights, and you know it."

She stood in the doorway and tried to think of a good answer. "But this is special, since Mayella's been gone all summer. And I'll be back in a minute to set the table—all right?"

"Only because the Crenshaws are probably expecting you," her mother said at last.

Salina hung in the doorway a moment longer. "No matter what else, Scooter Russell has got some crazy ideas."

She found her father and brothers at the paddock, exactly where she thought they would be, her daddy and Mark leaning against the knotty fence railing, watching Paul adjust Sugar-Boy's bridle.

"Hi!" she said.

Her daddy smiled and patted the top of her head. "Hey, gal. How was school?"

"Different. Y'all get anything in Sevierville?"

"More bills. Some things for the tractor."

"Oh."

Paul was leading Sugar-Boy around the grassy enclosure. Salina jabbed the ground with the tip of her shoe. "You'd think he would have the decency to come over and ask about the first day of school," she griped. "But no. He's too wrapped up in that horse." She glanced up at her father, hoping for sympathy, but he kept silent.

Mark climbed the fence and perched on the top

rail, the afternoon sun highlighting his red hair. "Sugar-Boy's beautiful," he said.

Paul strutted to the gate, Sugar-Boy close at his heels. "How do y'all like that? I'm not even leading him, and he's following me around like a pup!"

Mark hopped from the rail. "Course. You hog him all the time! Nobody else ever gets to do anything with him." He reached through the fence to pat Sugar-Boy, and the colt shied away.

"That's because you scare him. See?" Gently, Paul rubbed the colt's nose. "Isn't that right, Boy?" Sugar-Boy nudged Paul's side, leaving a dark wet spot on Paul's denim jacket.

"Looking for sugar," Salina commented. "Like when he was a baby. A foal."

Mark took Paul's hand and shook it. "When can we ride him? Huh? When?"

Paul's dark face colored. "Not for a long time, and you know it. He's fragile. I'll start putting weight on him in a month or so, but don't you dare try riding him till *I* say it's okay."

John Harris shot Paul a reproachful look. "Mark," he said, "Sugar was premature, and Paul needs to go slow with him. I'm sure you can ride him when the time's right—can't he, Paul?"

"Yes, Sir," Paul answered, his voice even, although his face was pink with embarrassment.

Mark pushed back his hair with the palm of his hand, studying the ground. Salina glanced at Paul, sideways. "I brought your lessons and the books you need for tomorrow. —Did y'all hear something about those surveyors while you were in town?"

"Not much," her daddy said.

"Ha," Paul added immediately.

Salina pressed no further. She didn't know much about Sand Lick Road, except that it ran in front of their farm. Turn right, and you were in Hogginsville. In the opposite direction, the road wound beyond Mayella Crenshaw's house, past Minnie Myrtle's store, and on to Pigeon Forge. Gatlinburg was off in the distance, hidden in the mountains. From that small tourist town Salina didn't know where the road went, and she didn't care. All she knew was that she did not like it when her father and Paul fussed with one another or even came close to it, which happened more often lately. She did not understand it. They had always gotten along. These new tensions made her uneasy. She glanced toward the house. "Reckon I better go help Mama with supper, else she'll be calling me."

Suddenly, Paul grinned. "What're we having?"

"*You're* having fried pork chops and mashed potatoes and gravy and biscuits, but I don't know what I'm having, 'cause *I'm* going to Mayella's for supper."

"That's too bad," he said.

"Mayella's?" Salina's daddy asked.

"Yes, Sir." She started hastily toward the porch.

"Tell your mother we'll be there in a minute," her daddy called to her retreating back, "and don't be making any more plans on school nights."

With her back to her father, Salina made a wicked face. "I won't, Daddy," she promised.

Something Salina particularly admired about Mayella Crenshaw's house was the living room. It had royal blue carpet and a sofa covered in blue velvet. On the wall above the fireplace hung a painting of a boy with bobbed hair and bangs, dressed in a blue satin suit. Soon after her wedding to Sam Crenshaw, Mayella's mother had ordered a kit and copied the picture in oil by number. Mayella's mom didn't paint pictures anymore— she was often sick. Or acted like it. Though Mayella had never said anything, Salina had heard Mary tell Hank that Rose Crenshaw was a hypochondriac. Looking in the dictionary, Salina had learned the word described someone who figured that if they weren't sick yet, they soon would be.

Everytime Salina walked past the wonderful blue and white living room, she caught her breath. Tonight, however, she had only a glimpse of it, because after supper Mayella was in a hurry to get upstairs to her bedroom. In addition to having a blue living room in a house high on the crest of a hill, Mayella Crenshaw was lucky in another way: an only child, she had a bedroom to herself and a good chance of keeping all her private stuff safe.

She followed Mayella into the bedroom and stopped short. Movie star photos covered the walls, Barbara Stanwyck, Tyrone Power, Jane Wyman. "Where in the world did you get these?"

"I bought every movie star magazine in the drugstore in Sevierville and cut them out. Aren't they just beautiful?"

"Everybody in Hollywood's beautiful."

"Uh-huh," Mayella went on, "and when I'm eighteen, I'm going to take the train and go to California and my picture is going to be on the cover of *Screenland*. I decided this summer."

Going to her closet, Mayella produced white majorette boots and a baton. The boots had silky yellow tassels. "I learned how to twirl this summer. If we had a band at school like my cousin Jim has in Sevierville, I'd be a majorette."

And if pigs had wings, they'd fly, Salina thought. Sometimes the way Mayella acted so stuck on herself disgusted Salina, even if Mayella was her best friend. "Yeah," she answered dutifully.

"See that picture of Jane Russell by my bed?"

"Uh-huh."

"I want you to fix my hair just like that." Mayella sat on the bench that matched her dresser and scooted toward the big oval mirror. "You can visit me in Hollywood."

Salina carefully combed Mayella's long black hair. "For a while."

Mayella glanced across the bedroom to a picture of Scarlett O'Hara and Rhett Butler taped to the wall. "Wonder what Scooter Russell's doing tonight? What a twerp."

"Who knows?" Salina answered. "Old stick-in-the-mud pessimists probably don't ever do anything. Except you know what?" she added, feeling suddenly inspired. "I bet she's going through some books looking for an unhappy ending."

Mayella grinned slyly. "Salina—don't you think Frank Talley's cute this year?"

Salina drew back. "*Cute?* What do you mean, cute?"

"*Salina,*" Mayella groaned.

"That's my name, don't wear it out."

"Salina, there's something different about me you haven't noticed." Mayella pulled out her blouse a bit.

Bosoms! Mayella had little bosoms! Quickly Salina averted her eyes. "When did *that* happen?"

"Well, not all of a sudden, silly. I got my period over the summer. And that's not all." Mayella opened one of the dresser drawers. "Look what Aunt Lucy bought me!"

Salina stared at the small piece of clothing dangling in Mayella's hand. "A brassiere," she whispered. "Do you really have to wear it?"

"*Have* to?" Mayella exclaimed. "Are you crazy? I can hardly wait! But Mama says I can't till I'm older." She grimaced. "Or at least, bigger."

"I am never going to strap myself in one of those things," Salina vowed soberly. "Never." And Mayella had said she had started having periods. Like Mary. Like she would, one day soon. "Let's talk about Hollywood," she said.

They sat on the floor resting their backs against Mayella's bed and looked at fan magazines and talked about Hollywood, where everybody—all the stars—lived in mansions and had servants. "Everybody has two swimming pools," Mayella said, "and they go to parties and drink pink champagne. Oh!" she squealed, shaking the magazine she was holding, "here's what I've been looking for, an old picture of Carole Lombard just before she got killed. And here's one of her and Clark Gable! I knew it was somewhere."

Salina took the magazine and closely studied the platinum-haired actress. "Carole Lombard," she read aloud, "who on a single day in 1942 raised over two million dollars for the war effort and died that night in a plane crash, flying home to California and her famous husband."

"That is so tragic," Mayella murmured. "No wonder he always looks so sad."

"I know," agreed Salina. "Look. She's wearing satiny white pants to go to a party at night. And look here," she added, pointing to a photo of Lombard and Gable resting on their heels before a stone fireplace, Gable stoking the dying embers, Lombard watching, a barrette holding her blond hair from her pensive face. "She's got on pants here, too. I bet she even wore them on Sunday."

"Slacks," Mayella said, her voice longing. "Dressy slacks."

Filled with envy for the glamorous movie star who married the King of Hollywood and wore anything she wanted, anytime she chose, Salina ran her finger over the picture and closed the magazine.

"Boyoboy," she said. "She sure was lucky."

* * *

That night, after Salina climbed in bed and wished Mary goodnight, though she was tired and spent, she lay sleepless for a time, her brain wide awake. Today Mayella had seemed different . . . itchy, somehow, and at loose ends. Other parts of the day did not make sense—the parts where Mary and Paul did not stay in place, and Salina felt let down and sorry. She had put them exactly where they belonged and they had popped back at her, like pieces in a jigsaw puzzle that just won't go, no matter how hard you squeeze them . . . and dumb old Scooter Russell was the biggest offender of all.

✃ *FOUR* ✄

*B*oys!" Miss Williams called, climbing from the front seat of the farm wagon that had driven the eighth-grade class high into the Sugarlands. "Girls!" She clapped her hands and organized the hike and picnic, and when the sun was straight overhead, they unpacked their sack lunches and ate, the boys balanced on boulders clinging to the mountainside, the girls nearby on faded quilts spread over the grass.

"Sure is peaceful up here," Abigail sighed.

Salina nodded, silently breathing in the sweet mountain air and the scent of wildflowers mixed with the smell of damp earth, feeling the quiet power surrounding them.

Frank Talley gave a short laugh. "You'd better enjoy it while you can. Once fall gets here and the leaves start changing, the tourists'll be on their way."

"That's right," Salina said. "They'll be thick as flies in a few weeks—great."

Abigail licked blackberry cobbler from her chubby fingers. "At least it doesn't affect us like it does the folks in Gatlinburg."

"It might not affect us *now*," Frank said, "but you just wait. Talk is there's gonna be a new road built."

Road? Salina pricked up her ears.

"My dad's heard stuff about that," Johnny Campbell said. "Why would the government want another road, Miss Williams? We've already got Sand Lick."

"Sand Lick Road is a secondary road," Miss Williams explained. "Some people think the state has plans to build a primary road, which would be a highway linking up large communities like Sevierville and Maryville."

Mayella frowned. "Why's there a fuss about a highway? Who cares?"

"Paul, for one," Salina answered with conviction.

"Highways spoil the land!" Frank Talley's Adam's apple bobbed in his throat.

"I know why people are against it," Salina went on. "Before we knew it, strangers would be taking over Pine Valley and changing things."

"Like what?" Scooter Russell asked.

Salina drew back, abashed. "You don't know about the mountains?"

"Of course not," Mayella said.

The other girl blinked, cocking her head to one side. "Sure I do. I love the mountains."

"Salina means the park," Miss Williams said. "It's been open eight years, and a lot of people dislike the changes that have come with it. The tourists, the traffic and activity."

"Not just the things that have come with it," Salina said with feeling. "Old Daddy—that was my grandfather—had to sell his *farm* to the park people."

"A lot of people did," Frank added.

Salina frowned at Scooter. "My brother Paul says that near Gatlinburg tourists pay money to see black bears locked in cages so small they can't turn around in them. Sometimes it's so crowded, you can hardly cross the mountains because of traffic. *That's* what happens when *outlanders* show up where they're not wanted." She gave the white-haired girl a pointed look.

"Salina," Miss Williams said, "strangers aren't necessarily terrible people."

Scooter had been quietly listening. "I bet if we did get a new road like that, my family could sell lots more produce and all the quilts we could make."

"To the strangers flocking in," Salina stated.

"That's right."

Scooter's attitude infuriated Salina. "I *knew* you'd be for this dumb new road."

"If it would make things better for my family, yes."

Salina erupted furiously, "And I suppose just phooey on everybody else!"

"Salina!" Miss Williams said. "That's enough."

Salina breathed deeply and pursed her lips.

"Since we haven't heard from the state government, I really don't think anything is definite," Miss Williams said. "At least not yet. And I believe that for now, it would be best to drop the subject."

"But what if?" Salina insisted. Anger seethed deep in her chest. "The mountains are so beautiful, and they've already been through too much change!"

"Please, Salina," Miss Williams said, and there was a little silence. "Now, since the class has shown such an interest in roads, I'm going to let two of you make land transportation the subject of your fall project. Any volunteers?"

Mayella took a quick look at Salina and waved her hand, while Salina sat thinking that land transportation was the last thing she wanted to do a report on.

"Why, Mayella," Miss Williams said, "how nice." She surveyed the group. "Why don't you and Frank work together?"

"Frank?" Mayella looked surprised. Then pleased, as she glanced in Frank's direction. "All right."

"Abigail, I think you and Johnny, and Salina—"

Her eyes swept Jolene and Willard and Cloyd. "You and Scooter. I'll assign the remaining topics on Monday or Tuesday. You'll have several to choose from."

Salina stiffened.

"Darn," Abigail complained, "I wish she'd put us together."

Salina made no comment. She was busy watching Scooter Russell from the corner of her eye, wondering how in the world she could work on a project with someone like her. Hooray for a highway, Scooter had said. Phooey on Rhett Butler and Scarlett O'Hara.

Sitting there on the mountainside, Salina decided that probably nothing would come of the road; anyway, she sincerely hoped not. As for Scarlett and Rhett . . .

On the way to the farm wagon, while the others ran ahead, she briskly tapped Scooter's shoulder.

"Salina," said the white-haired girl.

Salina regarded her defiantly. "I'm going to prove it."

"What?"

"That Scarlett and Rhett lived happily ever after."

Scooter looked simultaneously amazed and dubious. "How? Anyway, you can't, because they didn't."

Salina gritted her teeth. "Boy," she said before walking off, "are *you* gonna feel stupid."

During the ride home, Salina ignored her class-mates and racked her brain for ideas. Surely some-where there was proof—proof she could wave under Scooter Russell's nose. But where?

At first she could not determine whether it would be best to write Dorothy Dix at the newspa-per, or to Clark Gable. She was afraid Dorothy would guess she was a kid and give some kind of funny answer in her column for everyone to read, and Clark Gable—why, he got zillions of letters a day, Mayella's fan magazines said so; it would take too long to hear from him. Finally, the best idea came to her. She would not write either of them.

Early Saturday she went to Miss Minnie's store and waited for the bookmobile, and the minute it stopped at the gas pumps she raced inside and looked up *Gone With the Wind* in the card cata-logue. At home, she took a piece of the red-initialed stationery and sat at the kitchen table, and every time somebody nosed around, she cov-ered her letter with her hand and gave whoever it was a cross look till they took the hint and left her alone. She got a stamp from her mother, and when she finished addressing the letter, she walked to the end of the driveway to the mailbox and waited for the postman.

"Hey, Missy," he said when finally he came driving up in his blue pickup truck. "You got a letter for me?"

"Yes, Sir." Salina took one last look at the

address on the letter before slipping it into the
mail sack, then turned and walked back up the
drive, the words on the front of the envelope
dancing in her mind:

> To Margaret Mitchell
> *Gone With the Wind*
> The Macmillan Company
> New York City, New York

⇜§ *FIVE* ᐤ⇝

SALINA SLID BACK in the church pew. Across the aisle, she spotted Mayella sandwiched between her parents, Mayella taking peeks at Frank Talley, while Rose Crenshaw stared fixedly ahead. Salina leaned around Paul and cleared her throat, loudly, causing Mayella to look over her shoulder and cross her eyes.

Mary promptly whispered, "You'd better straighten up!"

"I didn't *do* anything," Salina protested beneath her breath.

"Is that right? So then why is Mrs. Orange staring a hole through you?"

It was true. Jimmy Don's rich grandmother had angled around in her seat to watch her. The woman murmured something to Michael Burmeister, who was beside her, and the young veterinarian turned to look at Salina Harris.

Hot with embarrassment, she fastened her eyes on the white-robed choir. Scooter Russell stood in the front row with her four blond sisters. Since the trip to the Sugarlands three weeks ago, Salina and Scooter had not spoken. In Salina's considered opinion, Scooter Russell was just plain weird. In addition to everything else, at noon most days Scooter stayed glued to her desk, her nose in a book while she ate her sack lunch, being antisocial. Which was fine with Salina.

She removed a paper fan from the slot in the pew in front of her and fanned herself vigorously.

"What are you doing?" Paul complained.

"What's it look like? I'm about to burn up!"

"You *are* gonna burn up if you don't behave."

"Page one!" Preacher Lyte called from the pulpit. " 'Holy, Holy, Holy!' "

Rising with the assembly, Salina sang cheerfully, "Holy, holy, holy, Lord God Almighty!!!" her eyes drifting back to Mrs. Orange and her companion, Michael Burmeister. After a minute, she punched Paul. "Why does he stay where he's not wanted?"

"Because Krauts are stubborn. That's what makes them dangerous. I wouldn't let him touch an animal of mine for anything."

Salina thought Michael Burmeister should go home to Louisville where he belonged. "We sure don't need him here," she said, and sang along with the others.

The vet's light brown hair was neatly combed, and he had on a white, long-sleeved shirt and navy pants. Not work pants, either, like Salina's daddy and brothers. His skin was smooth, his cheeks tinged with pink. He had a thin nose and delicate face. Salina murmured, "You know who he reminds me of?" Without waiting for an answer from Paul, she told him: "Ashley Wilkes."

"Ashley who?"

"You are so stupid," Salina said, and silently vowed *never* to tell Paul that Ashley Wilkes was Scarlett O'Hara's first true love.

Preacher Lyte said, "Brothers and Sisters, let us pray."

Salina folded her hands in her lap and closed her eyes, but she could not squeeze a prayer from herself. She was too busy thinking how sick and tired she was of checking the mail every afternoon after school. Three weeks was enough time for anyone to answer a simple question. How could writing one short letter take Margaret Mitchell so long when she had written such a thick book?

Salina was convinced she had done everything the proper way. She had gotten the publisher's name from the card catalogue, just as they all had in seventh grade when Miss Williams required everyone to write a letter to a famous novelist. She had been extra polite. She had been brief. She had asked the question straight out. She had told Margaret Mitchell the question was an important one . . . but should she have explained why? And that she was impatient these days, and restless?

Maybe that was where she had gone wrong. But one thing Salina knew: when that letter *did* arrive, she would parade around in front of Scooter Russell and wave it under her nose till that girl fell down on her knobby knees and *begged* her to stop.

Salina hurried down the church steps and took a full deep breath of cool mountain air. In the distance, vapors rose from the Smokies in pale gray wisps.

"Hey, Red!"

She whirled. Nobody called *her* that and got away with it!

Howard Gardner patted the top of her head, and instantly, she grinned. "Takes one to know one," she said.

A black patch covered Howard's right eye, which he had lost in the war. Howard worked at the Potts Lumber and Furniture Mill situated deep in Pine Valley. He was tall, six-three or -four, and skinny. Every time Salina saw him, she thought of a stick bug: all arms and legs. Events had moved swiftly for him and Scooter's sister, Sally: they were engaged to marry at Christmas.

"Hear you and Scooter's gonna be doing some work on Mr. Eli Whitney," he said. Eli Whitney, the man who had invented the cotton gin.

Salina was surprised Scooter had mentioned the assignment to Howard. "Looks like we are. Miss Williams put us together."

"I'm glad she did. Scooter spends too much time off by herself, to my way of thinking. She needs a good friend."

Friend? Salina thought. Sally's Howard sure had gotten the wrong idea. She and Scooter Russell would never be friends. "We haven't talked about it. But tell Mrs. Russell she'll be seeing me around." Unfortunately, Salina added to herself.

"Will do!" Howard started toward the small group of men gathered in the gravel parking lot beside the church. Salina's daddy and brothers were with the men. Mayella was nowhere in sight, and her mother and Mary were standing on the church steps, socializing.

"I'll tell you one thing dead certain," Homer Joiner said as Salina drew close to the group of farmers and slipped between her daddy and Paul. "If they build a primary road through here, this little town'll be ruined!"

Willard Cates, the undertaker, and his wife were getting into their car. "Homer," Mr. Cates said out the window, "a new road might generate business. Lord knows we need it, after the Depression and war." The couple drove off.

"They're both right about one thing," John Harris said to the others. "A new road would open up the town."

"Split it apart's more like it," argued Frank Talley's father. "Things are fine just like they are."

With a dead tree limb, Salina's daddy drew a small square in the gravel. "Times change, James Robert."

"Folks don't have to change with them," Mr. Talley returned stubbornly.

Homer dug a wad of tobacco from the pocket of his flannel shirt. "You mark my words, John Harris, that road's coming, and when it gets here, it'll take our farms, just like the park did!" He stuck the tobacco in his mouth.

"Cut through farmland?" Salina said. "That's impossible—" Her father glanced her way but didn't reprimand her. Salina looked at Paul, her heart pounding hard in her chest. His lips were pressed firmly together, his jaw muscles working as he clenched his teeth. Mark stood silently holding Paul's hand.

"Anyway," Salina's father said, sounding impatient. "This is all just speculation."

Just then Mrs. Orange, Michael Burmeister, and Jimmy Don passed near the group of men, and Homer took aim, spitting tobacco juice onto the gravel at their feet. "'Scuze *me*," he drawled. "I didn't know there was a lady passing." With glinting eyes, he looked pointedly at Michael Burmeister.

John Harris suggested quietly, "Maybe you ought to look *first* and spit after."

Over one arm the veterinarian carried a gray corduroy jacket. "Hello, Mr. Harris," he said with an easy smile. "Fine morning."

"It is that, all right." Salina's daddy shook the younger man's hand. "How's business?"

"Slim."

"It'll pick up. Day," John Harris said to Mrs. Orange. "How's Tommy?"

"Better, but he'll be in the Veteran's Hospital a while longer." For several months now, Tommy Orange had been in the hospital in Nashville.

"Mama went with Daddy in the ambulance a long time ago," Jimmy Don blurted. "Wouldn't let me go. Said I'm too young. Said I'd get in the way. Said I—"

"Hush, Jimmy Don," his grandmother told him gently. "Jimmy's seen his father just once since he was hospitalized," she added to Salina's father. "While he was still in Sevierville."

Salina didn't like thinking about Tommy Orange's automobile accident. He was thirty years old and was the president of the Hogginsville Bank and Trust, just like his father before him. And he had fought in the war against Germany and Hitler. She glanced at Michael Burmeister.

"Hello," he said pleasantly.

She stood absolutely still, unable to speak.

"Salina Faith Harris?" said her father.

"Hello," she murmured politely.

"Salina," the young man said. "That's a very pretty name." He smiled around the group of men. "You gentlemen send for me any time you need help with your stock—please."

He's embarrassing himself, Salina thought. She'd heard he came on the train from Kentucky and rented a room from Mrs. Orange, and that the woman had agreed to feed him if he would look after her terrier, Snoodles. Who can account for a vet-man tending a house animal instead of livestock? Salina wondered.

The trio passed on.

Homer Joiner snickered and spat, following

[54]

their departure with mean, squinting eyes. "Cain't y'all just picture that Kraut's shiny shoes in a pigsty!" Several of the farmers glanced John Harris's way. No one laughed with Homer.

That night, while Mary was still downstairs in the bathroom rolling her just washed hair in curlers and Salina's daddy was tucking Salina in bed, she asked him what he really thought about the new road.

"What new road?"

"*Daddy.*"

"Salina, like I said, anything we've heard is pure speculation."

"But, Daddy, everybody—"

"Salina," he said patiently, "we're not everybody."

She squeezed her toes in frustration and made a little murmur of protest, pulling the quilt to her chin. "But, Daddy, why do you think Michael Burmeister doesn't just go on home? Hardly anybody uses him. He's an outlander. We don't need him here." She thought of Scooter Russell. "We don't need any outlanders."

John Harris sat on the side of the feather bed. "If people don't use him, it's not just because he's a stranger. His people down the line are German —you know that."

Salina was unsure whether or not the fact that Michael Burmeister's family was German was as terrible as some people—Paul included—seemed to think.

"Since the war," her daddy said, "a lot of people don't care for Germans. City people, like in Louisville where German immigrants settled a long time ago, those folks don't mind, I hear. But Pine Valley's set in its ways."

Salina squinted up at him. "But the war's been over four years."

Her father stood, stretching a little. "That's right. Anyway, Burmeister can take care of himself. From the looks of him, he's done a smart job of that so far. He has had a few calls. And Mrs. Imy's renting him a room and feeding him despite the fact that Tommy fought in the war."

"How come, you think?"

"Wise people don't punish folks for things they had no hand in." He leveled his finger at her. "You stop fretting about it."

"I'm not fretting. But Paul says people like Michael Burmeister are dangerous and that he wouldn't let him touch an animal of his come hell or high water."

"Sometimes Paul has wrong ideas, too," her daddy said. "But nobody has to use Michael Burmeister if they don't want to."

"I wouldn't for anything. He's an outlander, pure and simple. But old Homer Joiner doesn't have to call him a Kraut. Especially not practically to his face. What's wrong with Homer, anyway?"

"Salina," her daddy said, and walked into the hallway, "if we could figure that out, we could solve most of the world's problems. Good night, girl."

❧ SIX ❧

SEVERAL WEEKS PASSED, and one starlit Friday, accompanied by Paul and Mark, Salina left the house and walked down the road toward the cabin where Scooter Russell lived with her grandmother. The late October moon lighted the night, softly illuminating the pumpkins and bales of hay dotting the fields.

"Sure am glad I wore my coat," Paul commented. "It's getting breezy."

Mark turned up the collar of his jacket. "Sure is."

Salina kept quiet. All she had on with her overalls and blouse was a lightweight cardigan sweater, but the chilly night air hadn't caused her dark mood.

Paul goosed her ribs. "What's wrong, sourpuss?"

"Nothing," she muttered. "Quit it! I'm really *excited* about studying with Scooter Russell tonight. —You ever seen where she lives?" In a brief exchange earlier in the week, she and Scooter had decided they would work on their report first at Scooter's, then Salina's.

"I've been through the valley some, you know that."

"And?"

"And what?"

"What's their place like?"

"Kind of plain."

Salina thought of Mayella's wonderful house. "I wish I was spending the night with Mayella."

"You do that every Friday night. You're in a rut."

"Maybe I happen to like ruts." She added glumly, "The Russells have an outhouse."

A devilish smile played at the corners of Paul's mouth. "Who cares?"

"*She* does," Mark said. "She didn't drink any iced tea at supper, and she went to the bathroom two times in fifteen minutes before we left."

"Do you *mind*?" Salina interjected loudly. "What are you, some kind of spy for the government?"

A pleased look settled on Mark's face. "Yes."

Walking single-file with Paul leading the way, they left Sand Lick Road, turned onto a narrow path, and entered the forest.

"It's dark," Mark said, touching his fingers to Salina's back. "I can't even see the sky—we got far?"

"You just keep up," she warned him over her shoulder, "and stay on the trail." She clutched the encyclopedia she had brought from home closer to her chest.

Paul said, his voice cutting into the night, "Y'all just wait. This is only the last part of October, and *Farmer's Almanack* says this winter's gonna be fierce."

"Ugh," Salina said. The *Almanack* probably was right. Hadn't they had their first killing frost in mid-September? And though there were some things about winter that she loved—like the first snowball fight and icicles hanging from the trees, glistening in the sunshine—she hated the blustering winter wind, especially when she had to walk to school against it.

Keeping a steady pace in front of her, Paul continued, "Best part about winter's spring. Spring always comes like clockwork after the bitter cold. Thaws things out and puts a warm glow over them."

All at once he halted, causing Salina to smack against him with full force. Mark plowed into her.

"Good grief," she began, then stopped, momentarily as startled as Paul by the panorama before them. With their backs to the forest, they stood on the edge of a plain lighted by the blue radiance of the moon. To the right lay a line of uneven, scraggy hills. Close on the left was a winding gorge. Beyond the gorge, farther west, the mountains showed black on the horizon. Salina shivered involuntarily, feeling suddenly very small: a tiny person engulfed in a huge, starry night.

About a hundred yards away sat one cabin and the foundation of another. Salina stared and blinked, peering through the darkness. Sally's Howard was building a place for himself and Sally to live in after the Christmas wedding. Next door, the shades were half-drawn. Candles flickered in the windows, upstairs and down. That was the Russell cabin, built of pine. Over the years, the house had weathered and turned silvery gray. By the light of the moon the cabin appeared small and lonely. Salina's stomach squeezed in on itself. She was certain traces of Scooter's father, Joseph Russell, must linger there, hidden in dark corners.

"Gosh," Mark said in a whisper, "this place sure is spooky." He slipped his hand into hers.

Paul straightened his shoulders. "Nah, it's just isolated. I've been through here during the day. It's pretty. Night's closed in, that's all."

"That's all? That's enough, as far as I'm concerned." Salina shifted her weight from one foot to the other, her eyes lighting briefly on the ravine winding past Scooter's cabin. In the moonlight, the ravine resembled a scar, a sharp blue cut between the plain and the mountains. She said airily, "I reckon you two can go home now."

"You don't want us to walk you the rest of the way?" This from Mark.

"Shoot, no," came Salina's reply, her voice big and brave in the night. "What do you think?"

He gazed complacently at her. "I think you hate this place."

In a good humor Paul said, "If the bogeyman gets you, don't blame us." The two boys turned away, Salina watching as hand-in-hand they vanished into the dark forest. Leaning forward, she turned an ear to the woods, but there was only silence.

The wind picked up. Holding the encyclopedia tightly, she tucked her head and struck out across the yard. Darn wind, she complained to herself, and darn Miss Williams, too! If that woman had one ounce of kindness flowing in her veins, Mayella and I would be laughing it up right this minute, but, oh, no—

"Whoo," an owl cried from the hills hovering behind the cabins. "Whooo?"

Salina halted, listening. In the moonlit shadows, with their skinny bare branches shaking and trembling in the gusting wind, the trees silhouetted against the sky looked crazy and wild, like skeletons dancing in the night. Behind her a twig snapped, sending her straight toward the cabins.

Dang! she thought as she hit Scooter Russell's stoop and then the front porch, if there is such a thing as a bogeyman, this is sure as heck one place you'll find him!

The door opened at once. "Hi," Scooter said, her manner direct.

Salina took an involuntary step back. "Hello."

Downstairs there were two rooms. The main one appeared yellow and dim to Salina's eyes. Beige candles burned in the windows and on the walls, stuck in wooden holders. Logs blazed in the fireplace. This part of the room was furnished mainly with a couch and several chairs. An intricate Star of Bethlehem quilt in shades of scarlet, orange, and blue hung from a rafter. At the opposite end of this area there was only a long wooden table and plain kitchen chairs. The kitchen beyond was dark.

Three of Scooter's sisters lay on their stomachs near the hearth with their chins cupped in their hands, studying by the light of the fire: Rachel, the youngest, and the twins, Jennifer and Josephine. Like Paul, Jenny and Jo were seniors at Pine Valley High School. The moment the girls spied Salina Harris they grinned. Granny Russell was sitting in a rocking chair near the fire, removing the strings from the green beans in her lap. She smiled, showing toothless gums, before returning to her task. Scooter's mother got up from the couch to greet Salina, putting her sewing aside.

Lena Russell was a slender woman with high cheekbones and thin lips, and although she was not old, perhaps thirty-five, gray streaked her light brown hair. "Come right in," she said. "I'll put your book on the table, and when you're all nice and warm, you and Scooter can go to work."

Salina gave the encyclopedia to Lena Russell, smiling brightly though she felt so wooden and out-of-place, and silently watched her return to the couch.

At the fireplace, she and Scooter stood with their backs to the flames, Scooter gazing straight ahead while Salina glanced around the cabin, racking her brain for something to say. Standing near shrimpy Scooter Russell made her feel awkward and gangly, like a big oaf or a giant. The couch, she noticed, was ragged. Someone had patched it with scraps of bright material— Scooter's grandmother?—and the sofa looked funny and sad.

"Nothing like a good fire, huh?" said Scooter.

"Sure isn't," Salina answered.

"A month from now, it'll feel even better."

Salina commented stiffly, "Paul claims this winter will be fierce."

"That Paul," Jenny murmured, looking up from her English book, and Josephine giggled.

"We're lucky this year," Scooter went on. "Sally's Howard builds great fires. He's out back right now, collecting more wood. Of course, Sally's with him. She hangs on him all the time." Scooter smiled. "Reckon we all do. Anyway, if you're ready, I guess we ought to get to work on Eli Whitney."

A short while later, Sally and Howard came inside. Walking through the kitchen with their arms loaded with wood, they found Salina and Scooter sitting at the table facing one another glumly, the encyclopedia closed between them.

"What's wrong?" Howard said. "Is it that boring?"

"No," Scooter answered. "It's just that there's not much of it, and Miss Williams says our report's eight pages, or else."

"Oh. Well, if you *really* can't get anything else done tonight, we'll just have to pop some corn and celebrate."

Sally crossed the room, and after arranging her armful of wood on the hearth, stood at the fire with the hem of her cotton dress hitched up, warming the backs of her legs. "Celebrate what?"

Howard smiled. "We'll think of something."

"Come on," Scooter said to Salina, and she pushed her chair back from the table. "That sounds good to me."

Celebrate? Salina didn't have anything to celebrate with these people. Certainly not with Scooter Russell. She was ready to say she thought she would just go on home when she looked outside the windows to where the forest was pitch black and spooky and decided it might be wiser to stay put and eat popcorn and wait for her daddy to fetch her at eight o'clock.

"Okay," she said, but without enthusiasm. "What's this?" she added as she stood up, noticing for the first time three initials and a date carved into the table top: JBR, 1941.

Lena Russell glanced up from the sewing in her lap. "Joseph signed the table when he finished making it, just like we sign our quilts."

Salina stood motionless, wishing she were not so stupid, sorry she had stirred sad memories. Then something crazy happened. As Scooter's mother told how they brought the table with them all the way from Signal Mountain, Salina heard joy in the woman's voice, like music. She stared at Lena Russell, her heart scared in her chest; how could joy and sorrow be in the same place at the same time? They could not, and yet . . . a thought came to Salina and danced away.

"That's nice," she murmured as the woman fell silent. Feeling foolish, Salina joined Scooter on the quilt before the fire, near Lena Russell's feet. The woman was sewing together large squares of un-matched fabric.

"What's that you're working on?" Salina inquired politely.

"A jacket for Scooter," came the reply.

"A *patchwork jacket?*"

Scooter said, "It's that or freeze." Glancing at her mother, hastily she added, "And anyhow, it's gonna be pretty. I can hardly wait to wear it."

Pretty? Salina thought. She seriously doubted it. "I can hardly wait to *see* it."

"It's gonna be different," Scooter agreed. "But that's okay—I kinda like being different."

Well, Scooter Russell, Salina's gaze said, so far, so good.

"It makes me feel special," Scooter explained, her small face open and serious.

Well, good grief, Salina thought, appalled to

hear the girl announce such a personal, private thing about herself. She glanced at the mantel over the fireplace, at the old clock slowly ticking away the minutes, and ran her fingers over the quilt beneath her. The quilt was black and pink and gray with touches of light blue. It had a black border and pink binding.

"This is pretty," she remarked.

Granny Russell smiled proudly. "Shadowed Squares. An Amish pattern. You quilt, Salina?"

"I'm working on one. But it's hard. I don't spend enough time on it, Mama says. I read a lot," she confided.

"Me, too," said Scooter.

"I know. Everytime I go to the bookmobile you have the book I want."

Scooter smiled.

"Patience is what it takes," Granny Russell said. "You've got to be careful and smooth out the rough parts. The joy comes later when you step back and see what you wound up with."

Rachel tugged her mother's sleeve. "We just gonna forget the popcorn?"

"Of course not, silly," Jenny said.

While Jenny led Rachel into the kitchen and started the popcorn, and Sally and Howard watched the fire, Scooter's mother took Salina and Scooter to the other end of the cabin. There she opened a cedar chest stacked with quilts and eased one from the bottom of the pile. "This is

Sally and Howard's wedding quilt," she said.

The quilt was predominantly white, with touches of yellow and green . . . the colors of spring, purity, and faithfulness. "Is this pattern called Steps to the Altar?" Salina asked.

Scooter's mother nodded. "Stand close so Sally won't see."

Scooter made a wry face. "There's not much chance of that. This place could burn down around us and Sally wouldn't notice."

Salina grinned, though she felt strange acting like part of this family. "Remind me to tell you about Mary sometime."

"I wrote this poem," Scooter went on in a low voice. "Miss Williams helped. I'm reading it at the wedding." The girl rummaged through the chest of quilts, then handed over a piece of notebook paper. "Here you go!" she whispered. Scooter clasped her hands, watching Salina read.

Rachel measured each stitch, taking her time,
Grandma made this quilt a fine design.
Then all of us sewed blocks in our own way,
To give this quilt to you today.
Mama joined the blocks, making the top,
And when the border was done, Mama stopped.
This quilt, you see, is white as snow,
And the border is yellow and green—
So when winter's hard and whistling low,
Pull it close and remember us and spring!

[67]

Slowly, Salina refolded the piece of paper and returned it. "That's nice," she admitted softly. "That's *really* nice. The wedding quilt and the poem, too, Scooter."

Rosy spots bloomed on Scooter's cheeks. "It's not what I planned at first. I had a special present all picked out, but what with the wedding being the same time as Christmas, I won't have the money to get it."

"What?" Salina asked, and she wondered, What could be better than a poem?

Scooter's blue eyes took on a wistful look. "A beautiful bottle of Evening in Paris cologne. All dark blue with a silver label. I saw it at Miss Minnie's. It's on the shelf with the fake finger-nails." She brightened. "But anyhow, thanks for liking my poem. I appreciate that. I—"

From across the room came the sound of Howard tapping the wooden floor with his boot as he flat-picked the guitar, playing "Sally Good 'Un." He glanced at Sally, smiling.

Lena Russell finished folding the quilt and put it back in the cedar chest. "Looks like we might be ready for that celebration Howard mentioned."

"On Friday nights," Scooter told Salina, "we make our own music—but on Saturday, watch out! We turn on the radio and listen to the Grand Ole Opry."

"So do we. I guess I love music better than anything, except reading."

"And writing those stories of yours. Miss Williams says you've got some good ones."

"She does?"

"Sure. She says we've got a lot in common."

Salina drew herself to her full height and straightened her shoulders. "Has she forgotten about *Gone With the Wind*?"

"I mean—" Scooter hesitated. "What with my songs and your stories. That's what I was starting to tell you a while ago. I value your opinion, and I want to read some of those stories of yours sometime."

Salina watched the other girl go to the fireplace, take up her banjo, and tune it. Stuff in common? she thought. You and me? What a hoot! She stopped. "I value your opinion," Scooter had said, matter-of-factly and sort of growny—like this was something serious. "And I want to read some of your stories." Other than her parents and Miss Williams, before tonight no one had ever asked to see anything she wrote—not even her best pal, Mayella Crenshaw. Not that she *cared.*

Further back in her mind, she caught the edge of another thought: not only did most of her friends dislike reading, few of them felt about music the way she did, while Scooter there . . . That girl, Salina thought, I bet that girl's got millions of songs circling her head, and I sure would like to know how hard it is for her to pin them down.

[69]

⤙§ SEVEN §⤚

SALINA, SCOOTER, and the twins were at the dining table, their attention on one of Sally's old scrapbooks, when someone knocked on the front door. Scooter's mother opened it, and John Harris strode into the cabin, his cheeks red from the wind.

"John," Granny Russell cried from her rocking chair, "go on over by the fireplace! It must be cold out there."

"Is brisk," he agreed, shivering despite his jacket and gloves.

Salina jumped up and drew him toward the hearth, slowing a bit when she noticed he was limping.

Sally's Howard stood to shake the other man's hand. "Leg bothering you tonight?"

"Just a tad." Salina's daddy smiled. "It'll get worse."

"It's going to be a hard winter—thank God cold doesn't bother this." Howard laughed, tapping his black eye patch.

Scooter's mother took John Harris's coat and gloves, and he joined the younger man on the couch. "We've had hard ones before." He held his bare hands toward the fire. "We'll survive."

Sally gave each of them a cup of steaming apple cider.

"Smells wonderful," John Harris said. "Thank you, Sally. The cup's nice and warm." He took a careful sip. "How're things at the mill, Howard?"

Before answering, Howard blew on his cider to cool it. "Fine. But come spring, I'm quitting the mill." The logs in the fireplace cracked and popped. "I'm giving myself over to farming."

Salina glanced at Howard, surprised by his declaration. Howard was well known for the intricate finishing touches he put on the beds and washstands produced at the mill. He also did small carvings of birds and animals. People thought of him as an artist; he was special in that way.

John Harris rolled his cup in his hands. His knuckles were stretched tight, the skin white and cracked. "Won't you miss working with your hands?"

Howard laughed. "I never thought I'd see the day I wouldn't be carving. But this can be a good, productive farm, John, and with Granny Russell's blessing, I plan to make it one. May take a while, but we'll make it."

"Howard's mind is set," Sally told Salina's daddy. "I think he should stay at the mill if that's where his heart is. But he's determined to make something of this place."

"He's like Joseph in a lot of ways." Lena Russell smiled, and Salina felt as if Scooter's father were with them in the room in a good, warm way.

John Harris thumped Howard's back. "If you need help getting started, just yell. Every man, woman, and child in Sevier County'll be here. By the way, the place next door looks good." He set the china cup on the floor. "Let's go, gal," he said to Salina. "We've kept these people up long enough."

Howard stood. "I have to leave myself in a little while. Thanks for the offer. We'll be doing a lot of planting."

On the way to the front door, Scooter handed Salina the encyclopedia. "I'll meet you at the bookmobile in the morning so we can see what's available on Eli Whitney. And I'll stop off at your house for a while on the way home so we can work."

Salina stared at the other girl, caught completely off guard.

"Bright and early," Scooter added cheerfully, and that settled it: within an instant everyone had waved them good-bye, and as if by magic, they were out beneath the stars, crossing the plain on their way home.

"Just look at the stars," Salina's daddy said,

laying his hand lightly on her shoulder.

She blinked her eyes against the wind's cold sting. "I wanted to go to the bookmobile alone in the morning, just like every Saturday."

"I know."

"That way, I get first choice of the titles checked in along the route during the week." Even better, she could run her fingers over the spines of the books she had previously read and consider the people within them in peace. Salina soothed herself by thinking that things could have been worse. In the morning, Scooter Russell's appearance at the bookmobile could have come as a complete, sudden surprise. And even if Scooter *did* drop off to study for a time, it was not like the whole day was unsettled. There remained the afternoon. That space of time when she would be alone to read or to go to Mayella's lay before her like a big square blanket with neat boundaries.

Still, she was bewildered and a little vexed because this had come about without her having one thing to do with it. Sometimes she felt like a piece of clay or a puppet people handled any which way they pleased, and she didn't like that at all. Especially when the person handling her was Scooter Russell.

She said peevishly, "Scooter didn't even have the decency to ask if it was okay for us to work together tomorrow. She just decided and announced her plan."

John Harris nodded. "That's true."

"Some people," Salina concluded, "have got a lot of gall."

"It'll be okay." Reaching down, he took her hand.

Salina smiled, though she was troubled. "See that batch of stars up yonder? Miss Williams is big on stars this year—constellations." Her breath puffed white clouds into the night air. "That particular one's called Aaron's Belt."

John Harris laughed softly into the darkness around them. "Orion's Belt, Salina."

Across the gorge, a train whistle sounded, hollow and low. Salina squeezed her daddy's hand and held it tightly. "Sometimes that sound makes me feel sad and lonely inside," she confided. "Even if somebody's with me."

"That's the sound of something leaving one place for another, and it is mournful, all right."

After a moment, she said, "Daddy, do you think Sally's Howard really wants to farm?"

"That I don't know, Salina."

"Howard plays music," she said affirmatively. "And he carves. I think he just wants to help the Russells."

"There's nothing wrong with that. Things change, Salina. People, too."

"Mayella's changed," she said, surprised by her own words. "She came home from Sevierville a different girl."

"You're still friends, aren't you?"

"Daddy," Salina protested, "what do you think? We're friends forever."

"What about making new friends? Especially with someone who's already a little different?"

He meant white-haired Scooter Russell. Salina said drily, "Why go looking for trouble?"

He laughed. "Salina, Scooter seems like a nice girl."

"She's stubborn about a lot of things," Salina informed her father. "For one thing, she doesn't care how many strangers come around messing up the mountains as long as her family can sell them a few quilts." She didn't mention the controversy over Scarlett and Rhett. "Even with Howard and Sally right under her nose, she probably doesn't believe in love at first sight. On top of everything else, she's pushy."

"I see," her daddy said.

Salina glanced skyward and wished on a falling star. "If I were Howard Gardner, I'd stay at the mill and say phooey on the farm."

"Ah." He nodded slightly. "You would."

"Yes. Did I tell you Jenny said Howard's going to build an addition on to Granny's cabin for them, so they'll have more room? They're all real happy about that."

"I imagine so. It's nice they have him around."

"That's what Mama says, too."

The pathway into the forest lay dead ahead.

Salina glanced back, across the dying meadow, at the Russells' cornfield, its stalks withered and limp. Most of the candles in the windows of the silvery cabin had been extinguished, and in the moonlight the place looked shiny and small and sad. Overhead, the cold stars glimmered.

* * *

Coming out of the bookmobile with Scooter the next morning, Salina shivered and buttoned her navy sweater another notch. Pine Valley was in the midst of autumn, and the ridges of the Great Smoky Mountains were scarlet, purple, and gold. Soon, it would be Halloween.

The two girls followed Sand Lick Road past viny wooden fences and farmland, Scooter Russell fanning the pages of a book on famous Americans. "This looks okay. With it and the biography Mrs. Tate promised us, we'll have plenty of material."

Wary, Salina answered, "That's if she can *get* it. If she can't, we'll have to stretch our report like mad."

Scooter gave Salina a quick, sly look. "You write big?"

Despite herself, Salina grinned. One thing about Scooter Russell: she had a way of making you laugh whether you wanted to or not. "I can if necessary. What else have you got there?"

"The Count of Monte Cristo," Scooter announced happily, "and I can hardly wait! It's always checked out. My name's been on the list for six

weeks. What did you get?"

"*The Black Stallion Returns*. You'll love *The Count of Monte Cristo*. I read it last year, and it's so good—"

Puzzled, Scooter said, "*The Black Stallion Returns?* There's another Black Stallion book? How'd you know that?"

"Mrs. Tate. She remembered how much I loved the first one. But you know what?" The words tumbled from Salina. "I've been saving it to read. I could have checked it out before now, but once I finish it, I won't have it to look forward to anymore, and—" In midsentence, she stopped. Never had she told anyone how tender she felt about books; who would she have told, anyway?

"Salina," responded the white-haired girl, "I know exactly what you mean. I love books, too."

Salina smiled, embarrassed and pleased.

The other girl ran her thumb beneath the shoulder strap of her faded overalls. "How do you like my new blouse? Mama made it from this month's flour sack material. I think it's nice."

"Mayella's mom got new storage room curtains out of that same print." Salina paused. They were approaching her house. At the end of the driveway stood the mailbox, black and dull in the midmorning sun. She dashed to it and checked the mail.

"What's wrong?" Scooter asked at once.

"Nothing." *Everything.* If the letter from Margaret Mitchell had come today, she could have read it to Scooter Russell and settled things about Rhett

Butler once and for all. Instead, greatly disappointed, she looked over the thick letter addressed to Mary and the bill from Montgomery Ward. "I was hoping the new Monkey Ward catalogue would be here," she fibbed. "But it's not."

"With all the Christmas items," Scooter said. "Gosh, I love that stuff so much. Not that I ever get any of it. Santa Claus—ha." She lapsed into silence and with the tip of her scruffy shoe made a random design on the road's hard surface.

"Well," Salina said, for lack of anything else.

They started toward the house. Mark was alone on the front porch, playing a game of jacks, Salina's old blue stocking cap pulled close around his eyes. A gust of wind shook the trees, and a shower of leaves fluttered to the ground.

Just as Scooter handed Salina a yellow maple leaf laced with scarlet, Paul wandered on to the front porch.

"What are you two doing down there?" If seeing Scooter Russell with his sister surprised him, Paul did not show it.

"Admiring the leaves the wind's blowing around," Salina replied. "Look at this one. Scooter found it. Isn't it pretty?"

Paul addressed the other girl: "A beauty."

"Where'd Mark go?"

"Inside." Paul grinned. "He's making cornbread for dinner. Are you going out back to see Sugar-Boy?"

Salina frowned. "We're going inside to work on Eli Whitney."

"You like horses?" he asked Scooter.

"Sure," the white-haired girl told him. "A lot!"

"You know we have one?"

"Paul," Salina interjected impatiently, "everybody in Pine Valley knows about Sugar-Boy."

"Want to see him?"

"Sure," Scooter answered, "but from what I've heard, he's not likely to let me near him."

Paul bounded down the steps. "He will if *I'm* around." He started for the paddock with her, chatting easily about Sugar-Boy, explaining how weak the colt was at birth.

Salina stared after them, her mouth hanging open. Paul was acting so nice, bending down a bit, hanging on Scooter's every syllable and talking up a storm. Before he had never given her friends the slightest notice—and one friend in particular he always took great pains to ignore.

She hurried to catch up. The two girls fed Sugar an apple and ran their hands gently along his sleek neck while Paul leaned against the fence and watched, smiling lazily, one long leg across the other.

"You know, Salina," he said after a bit, "I've been thinking—"

"Don't hurt yourself," she responded automatically.

"—next week, Sugar'll be a year old."

"And you want to give him a birthday party."

"Ha, ha. No, when I finally start putting weight on him, I'd like your help. He should be completely broken by the first of the year. This spring, we'll be riding him all over the place."

Astonished, she stared at Paul: "You want my help?"

"Sure. You can keep him calm by talking to him while I get the sandbags on him. Mary's not interested, and Mark would just be in the way; besides, you have an easy touch. Sugar likes you."

As if agreeing, Sugar-Boy playfully nipped Salina's wrist.

"Well," she said, feeling a rush of warmth for the horse. "Well," she said again, genuinely delighted.

"Right now," Paul said, "I'm starving."

"Starving," Salina scoffed. "And I'll bet it's not even ten-thirty! You may as well have dinner with us," she added to Scooter, feeling generous as the trio walked across the yard toward the back porch. "That way, we can work till noon. But it's meat-loaf. Your mama be worried?"

"Nah," Scooter grinned. "I told her I'd be staying."

Salina's smile froze, and she paused for one instant before pushing open the door to the screened-in porch.

"Lord, these soup beans are fine!" John Harris said during the meal. "Aren't they fine, son?"

"Yes, Sir, they are." Paul was ready for seconds.

He crumbled a piece of the cornbread baked by Mark onto his plate and ladled white beans on top, then sprinkled sugar on his stewed tomatoes and served himself another thick piece of meatloaf.

Salina took the meat platter. Working together for almost two hours, she and Scooter Russell had managed to do a lengthy, if incomplete, outline on the life of Eli Whitney.

"You want some more beans?" Paul asked Scooter.

"Sure. I love soup beans."

"How about some homemade relish? It sure beats Salina's catsup."

Everyone laughed. Everyone except Scooter, who gave Salina a sympathetic look. But now Salina was beginning to think maybe the main reason Paul had requested her help with Sugar-Boy was to impress Scooter. "What did old Hanky-Boy have to say?" she asked Mary with a frown.

"That," began her sister, "is private information, and I'll thank you to leave my letter alone!"

Salina bristled. "I wouldn't touch your stinking old letter and you know it!"

"Girls," Anna Harris said in a warning tone.

After dinner, John and the boys stacked their plates on the counter and went outside to do the afternoon chores. When the dishes were washed and dried and the kitchen floor swept, Scooter said, "Well, Salina, I think we've done enough studying for one day. Want to—"

"I'm going to Mayella's," Salina said quickly.

Alone, her tone implied.

"Oh." Scooter smiled. "All right." She got her library book and thanked Anna Harris for the meatloaf, Salina silently listening and tracing her finger around the side of the half-eaten chocolate cake on the counter—making mouse tracks, her mother often said.

Scooter looked at Salina: "We could walk together as far as your mailbox."

Good *Lord*, Salina grumbled to herself. "I've got something to do first," she said.

"Okay—see you in the morning." Finally, Scooter headed for the front porch.

"Sure." Salina watched the other girl skip lightly down the steps before closing the door with a muffled bang, certain that for the rest of her life she was going to be haunted by pesky little Scooter Russell.

ᵉᔥ *EIGHT* ᖰᵉ

O NE WEEK LATER, the Harrises piled into the green pickup truck and headed for the Crenshaw's Halloween party. Before John Harris brought the truck to a full stop at the bottom of Mayella's gravel driveway, Salina and Paul jumped from the back and raced up the hill, deserting Mark and the bright orange pumpkin beside him in the truck bed. During the week, working alone, he had carved the pumpkin a smiling face and cut a hole big enough for a little boy's head in its top side. Before leaving the house tonight, he had pulled a white sheet on over his clothes.

Tiny yellow lights twinkled in the trees. The paper lanterns Mayella's Aunt Lucy had brought from Sevierville swayed in the night air. Thanks to a break in the weather, the evening was cool, but not unpleasant; Salina and Paul had left their coats in the pickup truck.

Sally's Howard and the other musicians were

playing a bluegrass tune, grinning as one dancing couple after another laughed and sat down. Near-by, Mayella and Jolene stood watching Sam Cren-shaw and a blond-headed boy stir the sugary mixture they were cooking for the kids to pull and eat later in the evening.

That must be Mayella's famous cousin, Salina thought.

"Salina!" a now-familiar voice called over the sound of music as Salina hurried past the band toward her friends.

"Scooter." In the past week, Salina and Scooter had spoken but hadn't spent any unnecessary time together.

The white-haired girl clasped her hands behind her back. "Nice party, huh?"

"I just got here . . . What did you bring?"

"Fried chicken and mustard greens. Mom killed five of our best chickens this morning."

"Sounds good," Salina said, and made motions of moving on. Mayella was watching them, wearing the white majorette boots and casually twirling the baton in her fingers. Over her dress she had on a new white jacket made of rabbit fur. Lord, Salina thought.

Scooter continued, "How come y'all are so late?"

"*Mary*," Salina groaned. "We had to wait for her dumb hair to dry, then she couldn't find her new ribbon, and we conducted this *huge* search for it all over the house."

Scooter grinned knowingly. "Sally's always taking forever to get ready. Jo and Jenny, too—especially Jenny."

There was a break in the music. "Oh, Sa-liii-na!" sang Jolene from Salina's left, and Mayella squealed gleefully.

"Well," Salina began.

"Guess what?" Scooter said.

"What?" Salina's eyes strayed to the other girls.

"I finished *The Count of Monte Cristo.*"

"You did?" *The Count of Monte Cristo*—that was a thick book, three hundred pages at least. And Scooter had read it in a week?

"So I wanted to ask when you'll be through with *The Black Stallion Returns.* Mrs. Tate said you didn't check it back in today. She said you weren't at the bookmobile."

"I've been busy helping Mayella plan this party." During lunch and walking home from school . . . but Salina had not spent any time with Mayella fooling around at the Crenshaw farm. "Mom's not feeling good these days," Mayella had explained in an irritated tone.

In the back of Salina's mind lay the nagging thought that Mayella might not be truly sorry she couldn't have Salina over—Mayella had probably spent the afternoons in the yard, wearing her white majorette boots and practicing the baton; for that, she didn't need Salina Harris.

From the tail of her eye, Salina saw a few kids bobbing for apples. "Mrs. Tate manage to get that biography for us?"

"Yep. We can add some stuff to our outline and start writing this week. Will you bring *The Black Stallion Returns* to church in the morning?"

"Salina!" Mayella yelled.

"Sure," Salina promised, and without another word, turned away.

"Ouch!" she heard the blond boy cry as she ran up to her friends. A bit of the boiling sweet mixture in the black iron pot between him and Sam Crenshaw had popped onto his hand.

"It's about time." Mayella shook back her long dark curls. "What was *that* all about? Was Scooter telling you about some pessimist book she's reading?"

"We were talking about *The Black*—"

"Jimmy," Mayella cut in, "this is my best friend, Salina Harris!"

Jimmy blew on the back of his hand and glanced at Salina, smiling at her with square white teeth and pale blue eyes. "Hi," he said lazily.

"Hi. Pleased to meet you." Mayella's cousin was bigger than Salina had imagined from his picture in the annual, and he was, she had to admit, cuter than she had at first thought.

"Salina," Mayella said, "how do you like my new coat? Aunt Lucy brought it to me!" She tossed the baton into the air over her head, caught it in her fingers, and to the delight of the small children standing nearby, rapidly twirled it.

I'd like it better on the rabbit, Salina thought. "Looks warm," she answered.

"Candy's about ready," Mr. Crenshaw announced. "Jim, why don't you go inside and ask Rose for some more plates?"

"I'll help!" Mayella said, her green eyes shining, and off they went, leaving Salina and Jolene to help stir the candy.

When the taffy reached the correct temperature, Mayella's father poured it carefully onto the few plates readily available. Most of the younger kids stopped their games and ran to grease their hands and choose pulling partners. When the candy was cool enough, they would scoop up a ball and pull it between them into long golden ropes, careful not to let the swinging, hardening candy touch the ground. When it was finally ready, they would cut the candy into bite-sized pieces and eat some of it.

"Easy at first," Mr. Crenshaw warned. "It's awfully hot."

Mark and his friend Mandy Phelps slowly made their way to Salina. Slowly, because Mark had put the pumpkin he had carved on over his head, and Mandy was leading him by the hand. Salina bit her lip, amused and exasperated. Mark had not planned ahead. The pumpkin's expression was upside-down, the mouth a frown across Mark's forehead.

"Mark," she said, "you didn't—how in the world did you get that thing on?"

"It's not a thing," he said, his voice muffled.

Salina gave the kids who were standing around

snickering a threatening look and helped Mark remove the pumpkin, then she took the black and orange eye-mask from his pants pocket and put it around his neck, so he could wear it later. It dangled there, a Halloween necklace. "Have you two had supper?"

"Yep. Mandy and me tested all the cakes. Till Mama and Mary made us eat some chicken and corn."

The little girl standing beside him nodded, her brown eyes wide.

"I'm gonna go find my sister," Jolene said, and started for the Crenshaw's back porch.

"If you see Abigail, tell her where I am." Salina dropped to her knees on the cool ground and coated Mark's hands with soft butter.

"You gonna pull candy with us?" Mark asked.

Salina wiped her hands on a paper napkin. "I'm starving for some real food." She whapped his bottom, lightly. "Have fun. And don't eat too much taffy, or you'll get sick."

At the picnic table, Salina piled her plate with sliced ham and green beans, corn lightbread, and a big slice of chess pie.

"Aren't you hungry?" she asked Abigail. Salina had bumped into Abigail on her way across the yard. The other girl's plate was almost empty.

"I'm on a diet," Abigail complained. "Mama says I have to."

Salina gave her the once-over. "Good."

The band, with Sally's Howard out front, playing fiddle, broke into "Billy in the Low Ground," and couples got up to dance. Salina's hands were full, her plate in one, a plastic tumbler of iced tea in the other. She nodded toward the music. "Let's go watch."

As they settled onto a bench, Abigail inquired seriously, "You going to dance?" and snatched a piece of Salina's ham.

"Sure, but only if Fred Astaire asks me." Salina's eyes skipped over the gathering. Near the band stood Scooter Russell with the twins and Rachel. Scooter was watching the banjo player with rapt interest.

"Gosh," said Abigail, "look who's coming."

Walking up the driveway into the light were Imy June Orange and her grandson, Jimmy Don. With them was the veterinarian.

"Good grief," remarked Salina with a trace of irritation in her voice. "What's Michael Burmeister doing here?"

"The Crenshaws must have invited everyone from church."

"Why does he keep hanging around? It's dumb."

Abigail slid closer to Salina. "Look over there."

Scooter Russell had borrowed a banjo from one of the musicians and was tuning it while Sally's Howard lowered one of the microphones. "Danny Creighton and Scooter are going to play a banjo duet," Howard announced to the gathering. "Y'all get ready—this is a good, fast one. And we all know Danny's fine reputation."

"Uh-oh," Salina murmured to Abigail. "Where's Mayella?"

Before Danny and Scooter were halfway through the instrumental, Mayella flew from the kitchen, moving straight for Salina. "Who gave Scooter Russell permission to play at *my* Halloween party? What kind of a mean trick is this?"

Salina and Abigail regarded one another in silence. All around them, people were clapping along with the music. Scooter was keeping up with Danny and doing some fancy fingerwork herself. Jim Johnson had followed Mayella outside and was standing on the sidelines, watching the performance.

"Guess they just figured it would be okay," Salina ventured.

"Well, it's *not* okay," Mayella complained loudly. "Scooter Russell has got a lot of nerve! I hate that girl!"

"Oh, boy," Salina said, watching Mayella stalk toward her daddy and cousin, the yellow tassels on her white boots jerking with Mayella's every step, the front of the rabbit jacket flapping open.

As Scooter and Danny stepped away from the microphones and bowed, the gathering applauded enthusiastically.

"Wow," Abigail said, clapping along with the others, "Scooter sounded great."

Like on the Opry, Salina agreed silently. Special, somehow.

Scooter made her way through the crowd; when she drew near the picnic tables, Abigail shouted and motioned her over.

"Hey," Scooter said.

"Hey," Salina replied.

"Weren't you scared to death?" exclaimed Abigail.

"I was, but then we started playing and I felt real good and forgot about it."

Looking past her, Salina saw Jim Johnson speak to Mayella, then turn and stride toward them.

"Good Lord," Abigail breathed. She straightened her dress. "Mayella's cousin's on his way over here!"

Jim greeted them politely and offered Scooter his hand.

She cut her eyes to Salina, then Abigail. Finally, to the boy, in a whisper, she said, "Is something wrong?"

"Not unless you just don't want to dance with me."

Scooter stared up at him, dumbstruck.

"Go on!" Abigail gave her a push.

Scooter Russell and Mayella's cousin danced around the grassy square, past the band, cutting into the shadowy corners and out again, into the golden light. Once, the boy swung her high into the cool night air, and she laughed, her hair the color of gold in the dissolving light.

"Would you look at that?" Abigail said, grabbing Salina's arm. "Scooter can dance, too! Isn't it wonderful?"

Salina said nothing. She was not so sure. She had seen the sour look on Mayella Crenshaw's face.

◆§ NINE ﴾◆

PAUL DRAPED a worn Army blanket over Sugar-
Boy's back. "There," he said as he ran his hand
over the colt's rump, "now you're all set." Sugar-
Boy's skin rippled beneath Paul's gentle fingers.
"And as for us," Paul continued, regarding Salina
and Mark, "if we don't get moving, we'll be late for
school." Quickly he closed the gate to Sugar-Boy's
stall and got his books off the barn floor.

On Saturday night, while Pine Valley lay sleeping, as though the Crenshaw's Halloween party
signaled the end of one season and the beginning of
another, they had had a light snowfall. This morning, the sun was shining and the whole world
glistened.

"Jeepers," Mark said as they tromped down the
driveway, "today sure is pretty."

When they were on Sand Lick Road, Paul stuck
the tip of his finger into his mouth, then into the

freezing air. "Wind's blowing south," he announced. "Know what-all I'm buying Sugar-Boy one of these days? A leather halter, a fine saddle, and a blanket; a fancy warm one fit for a Kentucky racehorse."

"Just where are you getting the money for all that?" Mark asked, giving Paul a skeptical look. "You could save your allowance forever and *never* have enough."

"He'll think of something," Salina said. "You wait." On Saturday Paul had asked her to help with Sugar, so she finally knew his earlier request was sincere; and yet, with her he remained sometimes impatient, and she still ached for the good old days.

Usually Mayella joined them as they passed her drive; today, there was no sign of her. The house on the hill was quiet. Sam Crenshaw's truck was gone. Salina didn't blame Mayella for not waiting this morning. "Brrr," she said, her teeth chattering, and pressed her books close to her chest.

With a flick of his thumb, Paul indicated the house. "What was the Queen Bee so fired up about yesterday morning?"

Salina puckered her brow disapprovingly. Sometimes Paul had such a smart mouth. After church yesterday morning, she had seen Mayella only briefly. Jim Johnson and his family were with the Crenshaws, and they were eager to start the twenty-mile drive home. "Guess what?" Mayella had crowed, passing Salina and Abigail on the church steps. "We're going to Sevierville for Christmas! Aunt Lucy's taking Mom and me shopping, and Jimmy's taking us to the movies! I'll tell you all about it at school tomorrow!"

Salina had remained on the church steps with Abigail, feeling slighted, somehow, and confused. Why would anyone want to leave home at Christmas? Besides, she and Mayella always had such a good time at the church party on Christmas Eve— had Mayella forgotten that? Mayella was abandoning her. That certainty made Salina feel sick inside. "I need to give Scooter Russell *The Black Stallion Returns*," she had said to Abigail without much enthusiasm, then had wound up going home with Scooter for dinner and to work on Eli Whitney for the remainder of the afternoon.

"If by Queen Bee you mean my friend Mayella," Salina said now, "her family's going to Sevierville for the Christmas holidays and have a wonderful time."

"Huh," Paul said, and she would have sworn that beneath his breath he added, "good riddance."

In class, after giving Abigail a wave and hanging up her jacket, Salina went to her desk. Miss Williams was in the hall, talking with the principal, and the classroom was noisy. With her spelling notebook, Salina smacked the top of Frank Talley's head, then she tripped over Cloyd's feet and fell into her desk with a thud.

Indignantly she snapped, "Why don't you watch

where you stick your big fat feet?" She glanced at Mayella and grinned.

Mayella punched Frank. "You see that?" she said, in a high good humor and laughing. "Salina—" She stopped, wide-eyed, the smile dying on her lips.

In the doorway stood Scooter Russell, wearing for the first time the patchwork coat her mother had sewn for her from squares of red and yellow cloth. Like Scooter had predicted the first night Salina went to the Russell cabin to study, the patchwork coat certainly was different. Funny-looking, somehow. Sad and cheery at the same time.

"Holy cow," Mayella said loudly, "a rag coat! I'd rather freeze than wear something like that!"

Salina sucked in her breath and quickly glanced in Scooter Russell's direction, uncertain whether, over the conversation of the others, the girl had heard Mayella's remark.

"My mom made this coat," Scooter said. "And I'd rather wear it than a dead rabbit *anytime*." She went to her seat at the back of the room, pink-faced.

"Well, *brother*!" Mayella huffed.

Salina remembered the candle-lit cabin and the tapping of Howard's boot on the wood floor. She remembered that when everyone at the kitchen table had laughed at Paul's joke about her catsup, Scooter had been on her side.

[96]

"I like the coat," she announced in a voice that carried around the room. "I think it's pretty." That was fudging a little; but the coat did look nice on Scooter.

"What!" Mayella snapped. She turned to Frank Talley, her cheeks blazing. "I got our road outline done yesterday—"

The bell rang, signaling the beginning of class. "All right," Miss Williams said on her way into the room, "page eighty in your geography books."

Salina opened her geography book, but she could not concentrate on Antarctica's hostile environment. She felt Scooter's presence behind her and knew without looking that the white-haired girl was sitting near the stove for warmth. And Salina wondered exactly how angry she had just made Mayella Crenshaw.

✑§ *TEN* ⧉✑

MAYELLA DID NOT speak to Salina again till Sunday night. "Want to sit with me down front?" she asked as the Harrises came inside the church. They were early, and the preacher was turning on the lights. Outside the windows, the mountains grew dark.

That morning, when Brother Lyte had introduced the guest preacher from Knoxville, reminding the congregation that it was time for the winter revival, Salina had perked up a little. In addition to fiery sermons, the revival practically guaranteed five nights of joyful gospel singing.

"Sure!" she answered with melting relief. Sitting side by side in the wooden pew, as the moon rose over the Smokies, she and Mayella sang with apparent content, Salina trying to ignore the funny rebel feeling lodged in one corner of her heart. The minute one part of her convinced her that she should admire Mayella for not holding a grudge, another part reminded her that Mayella hadn't had anything to hold a grudge *about*. Salina had not done anything wrong.

Then, in mid-November, a storm swept the mountains, covering Pine Valley with snow. Before long the sun emerged, the valley thawed, and when Sand Lick Road was passable, on the Friday after Thanksgiving, the surveyors came: three men in a green truck.

Salina watched from one of the living room windows as the men placed their equipment just a few feet from the yard. With so much going on lately—including the flare-up with Mayella—she had completely forgotten the road. She and Scooter had worked hard, keeping mostly to business, and turned in their project early, so they wouldn't have homework over Thanksgiving; when Scooter thanked her for taking up for her in class, Salina had shrugged, embarrassed, just wanting to forget the incident.

Too, she had spent considerable time making fruitcakes for the Christmas holidays with her mother, Mary, and Mark, while Paul spent his free hours in the barn or corral with Sugar. Paul had finally started breaking Sugar, using first one blanket, then several, then bags filled with sand draped across Sugar's back.

Now John Harris was on his way down the drive, and by the time Salina grabbed her jacket and ran outside, he was talking with the strangers, his hands on his hips.

"We're just getting a feel for the lay of the land," one of the men said, as Salina cut through the line of thick green pines separating the front yard from the road. Like Salina, his two companions stood slightly apart, listening. One of them was young, with fair skin and yellow hair.

"We're not getting much work done, though," the man continued. "Doing more talking with farmers than anything else."

John Harris said sharply, "Mr. Dury, folks have been hearing tales of a road coming through here since fall. Now you fellows come driving up."

"Well, like I've been telling everybody else, the way I see it, there's a good possibility the highway'll cut through here—"

Salina heard a click.

"The way I see it, Mister, that highway isn't cutting through *anywhere.*" Paul stepped from the pines, his shotgun leveled straight at the surveyor's belly.

Salina's heart skipped a beat. She had left Paul inside the house staring out the frosty windows with the rest of the family. Surely he . . . A cardinal flew over their heads, flashing scarlet wings. On the hills, snow glistened.

"Break that gun," John Harris said.

"No, Sir." Paul's hands were steady. He had been putting rabbits on the table since he was eight and went hunting around the French Broad River with Old Daddy. He was a good shot.

Salina was close enough to the surveyors to see that all three were terrified. They didn't know Paul like she did.

John Harris said softly, "What are you planning to do?"

Paul's long fingers coiled tightly around the shotgun barrel. His right forefinger rested easily on the trigger. "I plan to settle this thing right now. I'm tired of hearing road talk."

Mr. Dury glanced longingly at the state truck.

"Settle it by killing folks?" John Harris said. "Don't be ridiculous. All you're doing is getting yourself in trouble."

Paul put his free hand on his hip but kept the shotgun steady. "Daddy," he said, "you know I'm not shooting anybody! I want them off our land, that's all." He swung the shotgun around. "Y'all get on!"

Sugar-Boy was in the pasture. He neighed softly, the sound of the wind in the pines.

The men turned toward the truck.

"Stay put!" demanded John Harris.

The trio froze.

"That's enough," he told Paul, steadying his voice with an effort. Salina couldn't remember ever seeing her father so angry.

"These men are not on our property. Even if they were, you'd have no right to pull a shotgun on them. You're acting like a fool! You want to keep living on this farm, break it. Now."

It seemed to Salina they were frozen in place, her daddy and brother staring eye to eye. With his thumb Paul pushed back the breech. The barrel of the gun folded from the stock and hung limply across his right arm.

"Now we can talk," John Harris said.

"Talk!" shouted Paul. "What's there to talk about? You told the men at church the road's a good thing!"

"I said a new road would open up the town."

The yellow-haired stranger spoke. "Excuse me? I'm David Hoover. I think we need to get things into perspective here."

"What're you saying?" Paul demanded. "Why, you're not much older than I am!"

The fellow addressed John Harris. "What I'm saying, Mr. Harris, is that things aren't completely settled. The road is coming—that much *is* definite. The route it will follow isn't. We're just the second crew to come surveying the county. As soon as the Highway Commission gets all the facts together, you people will be notified. In the meantime, getting upset's premature."

"Huh!" Paul said.

John Harris looked thoughtful. "Paul, keep still. And you men go on about your work. We'll let you be."

"But, Daddy," Salina protested. "Paul's right! You should make them leave!"

"Hush, Salina. Go on inside." John Harris regarded David Hoover. "Premature or not, I plan to write the commissioner and tell him he's got some anxious people up here. May not make any difference, but I'll feel better if I try to do something."

Salina had not budged. Putting both hands squarely on her shoulders, John Harris said, "Go tell your mother everything's okay out here." Then he turned to Paul. "Now we're going in the barn to discuss being a hothead and making idle threats."

Salina went across the yard, resentment building in her chest. Her dad—why didn't he just *make* them leave?

At the porch, she stopped to look back. The three surveyors were fiddling with their gear, the peacemaker David pointing down Sand Lick Road as though nothing unusual had just happened. Why couldn't they just go away and leave Pine Valley alone?

Sugar-Boy trotted across the pasture toward the barn, stopped at the closed gate, and poked his nose over it, his breath blowing white puffs in the frosty air. His coat was furry now, for winter, and in the sunlight it looked nappy and dull, like brown velvet. As Salina had done, he looked back at the surveyors, then he whinied and shook his head, and he and Salina watched, sad-eyed, as Paul and John Harris disappeared into the barn.

That night, Salina had a dream that was rooted in memory. *It was a hot August night and they were at the county fair. They ran, she and Paul and*

Mark, ran from booth to booth, kicking up dust, and Paul shot a rifle, but not a real one, for prizes, while she and Mark watched, sucking purple snow cones.

What's this? Paul said, disappointed. He wanted the brown teddy bear.

Kaleidoscope! the big man answered, look here!

Paul looked, turned the small tube against his eye, and after a moment, he grinned. Look at this!

Salina looked.

No, me! piped Mark's little voice.

Salina looked, ignoring Mark. This tube about ten inches long shifted oddly shaped pieces of glass into new patterns as she rotated it, and these pieces were bright colors, they fell into a different brightly colored pattern every time she turned the tube against first one eye and then the other, a constantly changing set of colors into how many designs? A thousand? A million? Clearly, it was magic!

Oh, no, it's not, Scooter Russell sang in a lilting voice, just like I'm not white and blue, and in that sound that was Scooter, Salina saw more colors than ever she had imagined in that girl. Along with the white and the blue, for the first time in Scooter she glimpsed yellows and oranges and traces of scarlet. Then suddenly the scarlet flashed in Mayella, and in Paul, Paul, who had always been simple browns, and her daddy—abruptly, she woke and listened as something rustled in the woods behind the barn.

An owl perhaps, floating through the trees to a comfortable limb, a deer or a fox stirring in the dead of night? The dream forgotten, Salina relaxed and drifted back into sleep, for those were only the usual navy blue sounds of a peaceful country night.

* * *

"Salina," Miss Williams said when they were alone in the classroom the following Monday, "Thomas Orange is better."

Salina shifted in her desk and glanced out the icy windows, wondering why Miss Williams had asked her to stay after school. Everyone else was heading home for the day, laughing and punching each other, pulling on thick, woolen gloves and scarves. It was the first part of December, and the winter wind was freezing.

She regarded her teacher. "Mrs. Imy told Daddy at church a few weeks ago that Mr. Orange was making progress."

Rebecca Williams finished erasing the blackboard and sat down at Mayella's desk. "Tommy's still in the hospital, though. In Nashville. Jimmy Don hasn't seen him since he was transferred there from Sevierville. And of course Jimmy's mother, Janine, is in Nashville, too. She spends every day at the hospital."

Salina blinked, wondering what in the world this Orange business had to do with her. She should be home in the kitchen by now, telling her mother the news of the day and watching her fix supper. Tonight, they were having fried chicken; something Salina particularly enjoyed when they had fried chicken was picking the crispy part off the skin and eating it. She sighed longingly.

"Anyway," Miss Williams said, "now that Tommy's off the critical list, Janine feels Jimmy Don should be with them."

"Yes, Ma'am?" Salina drummed her fingers on the desk top.

"So, Jimmy's taking the train to Nashville in a few days. Since Mrs. Imy's back is bothering her, she can't go with him. He could travel alone, of course, but Mrs. Orange and Janine think it would be best for him to have company. Mrs. Orange and I discussed the matter, and I suggested you."

Salina stared at Miss Williams. "Me?"

The woman nodded.

"But how come? The Orange's have lots of friends! Michael Burmeister—that vet could take him!"

"Salina, don't panic. No one *has* to go with Jimmy Don. Mrs. Orange simply thinks it would be nice. You're a good student, you're responsible, and I thought you might enjoy it."

Enjoy it? Where would Miss Williams get a crazy idea like that? *Nashville*. Salina tried to picture herself in a city, but could not. "I've never been out of Sevier County," she said.

"It would be an adventure."

"I'm not looking for any adventures."

"Like visiting the Sugarlands in September. You enjoyed that, didn't you?"

"Yes, Ma'am," Salina admitted grudgingly. The sunlight streaming through the windows threw long, bluish-gold bars of light across the schoolroom. Motes swirled in them.

"If you decide to go," Miss Williams said, "Mrs. Imy's daughter, Agnes Prince, will pick you up at the train station in Nashville. She lives in Nashville, and you can stay at her house. Mrs. Imy will pay all your expenses, plus some extra."

Salina cut her eyes to Miss Williams. "Some extra?"

"Yes—and it's a tidy sum, too."

Salina's brain skittered over the Christmas presents she could buy with a tidy sum of money. And maybe one very special present: one of the things Paul had mentioned wanting for Sugar-Boy. She could give it to Paul on Christmas Eve, at the annual party held at church, and it would be the best surprise ever.

And yet—she squeezed her toes in the tips of her oxfords. "Nashville's so far off."

Miss Williams nodded agreement. "Over two hundred miles."

"Would Jimmy Don stay there with his mom?"

"Yes."

"Then on the way back home, I'd be alone?"

"Yes."

Salina scratched her forehead, and with her palm, pushed back a wisp of bright red hair. "What if somebody could go with me?"

"I suspect Mrs. Orange wouldn't mind."

"Mayella?" Salina suggested. She had spent the night with Mayella on Friday, and they had had fun listening to the radio and eating Thanksgiving leftovers. Mr. Crenshaw had mentioned that the surveyors had moved straight down Sand Lick Road after leaving the Harrises' and had told him the same news they had given Salina's father about the primary highway: it was coming, but the route had not been determined.

Miss Williams shook her head. "It would have to be someone who could afford to miss two days of school."

Salina sighed deeply in her throat. This year, Mayella's grades were worse than ever; she seemed in a perpetual stir and unable to concentrate. Any time they talked, Salina saw something unrelated going on behind Mayella's eyes. Abigail's grades were good enough for her to miss two days, but she sometimes bothered Salina's nerves.

"How about Scooter?" Miss Williams suggested.

"Russell?" Salina said.

"Her grades are always excellent."

"I know that, but—"

"But what, Salina?" Miss Williams sounded annoyed.

"If anybody had told me a few weeks ago I'd even consider going to Nashville and taking Scooter Russell with me, I'd have said they were nuts."

"I'm sure you would."

"But Scooter does need some money." You're the nutty one, said a voice in Salina's head.

"So taking her is practical," prompted the teacher.

"When would we have to go? I mean, if it's okay?" Salina reminded herself that the only reason she was doing this was to buy some Christmas presents. Missing two days of school wouldn't be so bad, either.

"The next train is this Thursday. Would you like for me to talk with your parents?"

Salina glanced outside. In a while, it would be dark. "No, Ma'am." She removed her jacket from the rack. "Miss Williams, how long does it take someone famous to answer a letter?"

"A while, I should think. Remember, last year some of you didn't receive answers at all."

"This is different," Salina told her. "That was just homework. This is important."

"Is that right, Salina?" Miss Williams looked amused, although she wasn't exactly smiling. "Anyway," she said, "if you can make the trip, I'll tell Mrs. Orange, and she'll wire Agnes."

"A wire with my name on it?"

"Yes. And Scooter's."

Salina let out a long breath. "I'll ask tonight."

She was halfway up the drive leading to the house, her gloved hands deep in the pockets of her jacket, thinking about the proposed trip to Nashville—an adventure? ha!—when she noticed Paul leading Sugar-Boy carefully across the back yard toward the barn. Sugar's head hung low. Every step seemed an effort.

She ran to them. "What's going on?" Paul didn't break his stride. "Paul—"

"I rode him," he said.

"You rode him?" Paul had continued the breaking process and had even gotten a saddle on Sugar. The horse was now over a year old, and he had done well so far. But Paul had sworn he would not ride him till January. "I'd rather be safe than sorry," he had said one afternoon when Salina was helping him with Sugar.

Now Sugar's sides were heaving, his nostrils flaring.

"Hold this." Paul handed over the reins and opened the barn door, his hands trembling. "I can't believe I did this."

Sugar sank to the hay on the stable floor, and Paul stroked his neck, talking softly to him. Then Paul got a few of the towels that were stacked nearby, and together he and Salina rubbed down Sugar's legs and sides.

"Is he warm enough?" Salina found Sugar's old Army blanket and covered him with it.

Finally, Paul said, "He's breathing easier. Right, Sugar?" Sugar-Boy raised his head a bit. Salina and Paul stood. "Salina," Paul said, giving Sugar another concerned look, "can I talk with you for a minute?"

"Sure." Uh-oh, she thought. Now what have I done?

"I mean and keep it secret?"

"I promise." Automatically, they crossed their hearts.

"I'm worried about me and Dad."

"Oh," Salina whispered. The idea that Paul had a problem or two unrelated to her had not occurred to her when she sometimes got upset with him.

"I'm afraid he doesn't . . . like me."

"Paul!" Sugar looked around at them, and Salina lowered her voice. "That's crazy. Daddy loves you."

"But it's like we don't get along anymore, and I can't help it. I don't mean to make him mad, I just can't stop. Like with the surveyors. I want to be calm, but I wind up yelling instead. Do you ever feel that way?"

Salina grinned. "All the time."

Paul smiled a little. "I was afraid it was just me." He bent down and stroked Sugar's nose.

"What about your friends at school? They're not perfect at home, do you think?"

"Who knows? I could never talk to anyone else about this kind of thing."

"Oh," she said again. Things hadn't changed between them, then; they had simply shifted a bit. Suddenly Salina felt lighter inside, like a great weight had lifted from her ribs. "Dad just doesn't want you to get in trouble or do something stupid, Paul. Underneath, he's still your dad. And maybe sometimes it's better to yell than explode."

Paul stood up, sucking in his breath. "Thanks, Salina. I think Sugar's okay. Let's go on inside."

They left the barn, going toward the house, and he laughed. "Remember your eighth birthday when Mom bought those balloons at Miss Minnie's?"

Together they had blown up the yellow and red balloons, then with one tucked under each arm, one in each hand, and one in her mouth, Salina had raced into the kitchen and let the balloons explode in all directions, scaring the others like mad.

"What a weird kid." Paul nudged her affectionately.

"You put me up to it," she said.

"Damn," he whispered, looking back toward the barn, "Sugar just wasn't ready. How could I have been so stupid?"

Salina followed him into the kitchen, where a fryer sizzled and popped in Old Mama's heavy iron skillet, wondering the same thing herself.

⧫ *ELEVEN* ⧫

*E*ARLY THURSDAY, John Harris drove Salina and Scooter to the railroad station. The trio sat elbow to elbow in the front seat of the rattling old pickup, Salina in the middle, Scooter by the window. She's looking around like this is some big event, Salina thought moodily; Scooter had been immediately enthusiastic about going to Nashville. A foot of snow had fallen in the night. Scooter had on a yellow wool hat with a ball on the end of the tassel; and though she had worn long underwear and a sweater beneath her patchwork coat, she was shivering. A grocery sack packed with toothbrushes and clean underwear, ham sandwiches, and fried peach pies for their lunch vibrated on the floor at the girls' feet. They had also brought along a couple of library books.

Paul rode in back. The roads were icy, and he had come in case they had trouble making it.

Bet he's freezing, Salina thought as they slid to a stop in the depot parking lot. Freezing and worrying about Sugar-Boy. Since Monday, Sugar had regained much of his strength, but his appetite was a bit off, and he craved water. Paul had, as it turned out, gone slowly with Sugar the day he rode him; the horse hadn't shown any signs of fatigue until he and Paul were on the way home. Paul had stopped immediately, removed Sugar's saddle, and carefully led him the remaining distance.

No matter what anyone said, though, Paul blamed himself entirely for Sugar's weakened condition. This morning before they left the house, Salina had accompanied him to the barn and helped massage Sugar's legs, giving him a little water, and as Salina watched Paul run his callused hands along Sugar's neck, tears stung her eyes, not because she was scared for Sugar, because she knew he would be all right, and not because Paul was hurting so inside, but because he loved that horse in such a big, beautiful way.

Guy Henderson was working the ticket counter at the train station. "Looks like you kids are it for today."

They thanked the man for their tickets, and at Paul's insistence, went back outside to admire the train.

John Harris indicated the road. "Here comes Jimmy Don."

Michael Burmeister was behind the wheel of Imy

June Orange's car. The instant the Coronet Dodge wagon stopped, Jimmy Don sprang from the back seat and ran up the wooden steps onto the platform, wearing a beige winter coat. As usual, he had on white knee socks and black patent leather shoes. Salina suspected that beneath the coat he had on the black velvet knickers he had worn to church on several occasions.

"You're taking me," he said, rudely pointing at her.

"Yes," Salina answered. "Scooter and me." Boy, did that sound weird.

Jimmy Don eyed the white-haired girl with distaste. "I've seen you in the choir." He squeezed up his pie-dough face. "That's the silliest name I ever heard!"

Scooter cocked her head, surprised by his pronouncement.

Mrs. Orange crossed the platform. "You be good now, Jimmy."

Paul pushed his felt cowboy hat back on his head. "I don't think the name's silly." He glanced at Salina, his expression sympathetic, then jumped from the platform and circled the Dodge.

Michael Burmeister smiled down at him. "Anytime you're in Hogginsville, drop by. I don't think Mrs. Orange would mind if I took you for a spin."

Paul turned his brown eyes on Burmeister and did not speak.

The train whistle shrieked.

"Yahoo!" Jimmy Don crowed. "I've never been on a real live train before, never, ever!"

"Me, neither," remarked Salina, "and I have a feeling I'm not going to like it."

"Hey," said the veterinarian, "you might be surprised. Have a nice trip."

Startled, she looked his way. He smiled warmly. "Thank you," she answered, and felt her cheeks go hot. "Guy Henderson's at the counter. He has Jimmy Don's ticket all ready."

"Thanks," responded the young man; grinning, he went inside.

Salina glanced at her daddy, and he smiled. "You'll be there before you know it."

"I know," she answered. "That's what worries me."

"Boy," Scooter commented excitedly, "is Sally ever going to be surprised! Evening in Paris—oh, boy."

"All aboard," shouted the conductor. "All aboaaard!"

"Come on, girls." Mrs. Orange took her grandson's hand.

Salina's heart fluttered in her chest, and she hung back.

"You two be careful," John Harris said.

Paul had come back up on the platform to say good-bye. Salina hugged her daddy's neck, then her brother's, and her daddy hugged Scooter while Paul studied his boots.

"*Girls,*" Mrs. Orange said anxiously.

"You'll be here tomorrow night?" asked Salina.

"At six," her daddy promised.

"Tell Mama and Mark I said good-bye," she called over her shoulder as they went to the train. "And Mary, too," she added at the last moment, but she couldn't be sure her daddy heard because the train whistle blew, Scooter almost dropped the fried peach pies, and Mrs. Orange whisked them aboard the train.

They settled into their seats, Salina and Jimmy Don facing Scooter. Several other passengers shared the car, a couple with a baby, and two young soldiers in dark green uniforms. Traveling where? Salina wondered, studying the two fellows surreptitiously. Fort Campbell Army Base in Kentucky? Sally's Howard had served there for a while when he was in the service.

Mrs. Orange dug into her purse and handed each of the girls a ten dollar bill. "You two are doing me a great service."

"Thank you," Salina and Scooter murmured.

Mrs. Orange handed Salina two more dollars. "The porter will come around with sandwiches. See that Jimmy Don eats." She gave Jimmy a kiss on the mouth and was gone.

The train creaked and strained to roll. Salina drew in her breath, bracing herself against the seat. On the platform stood her daddy and brother, Imy June Orange, and the young outlander; she waved, and the train pulled from the station.

"Here we go!" Scooter said enthusiastically.

Salina held her father and Paul with her eyes. As the train gathered speed, heading for the snowy, pine-covered mountains, and Pine Valley Station swooshed from sight, she gazed silently out the window, her heart contracting from a quiet melancholy, and a feeling of an illimitable loneliness.

Late that afternoon, the train entered the Nashville depot. The evening sky was clear, a cold wind blowing. On the platform men and women in heavy coats and gloves greeted the passengers, their breaths steaming in the cold air.

After pulling on her jacket and hat and gloves, while Scooter did the same, Salina picked up the grocery sack and Jimmy Don's coat. "Okay," she said to the boy. "Put this on."

She had guessed correctly about his clothing—Jimmy Don had on the velvet knickers.

"Yow," he cried, "Mama, Mama! Aunt Agnes!" Breaking past the other passengers, he ran down the train's narrow aisle and darted outside. Through the windows, the girls watched a young woman in a gray wool coat scoop him into her arms and kiss him. Salina recognized her as Jimmy Don's mother, Janine Orange, who was Rebecca Williams's age and close friend.

With Janine stood a slightly older woman. That must be Jimmy's aunt, Salina thought. Her name was Agnes Prince, and she was Tommy Orange's sister.

"This is Salina," Jimmy Don said when Salina and Scooter walked up.

Agnes Prince glanced at Scooter. "Then you—" Her smile wavered as she took in the girl's colorful patchwork coat and the yellow tassled hat. "You must be Scooter Russell."

"Yes, Ma'am," Scooter answered proudly.

"How can I ever thank you girls?" Janine Orange beamed at them. "Tommy's so much better now and misses Jimmy Don terribly . . . Scooter, you're new to Pine Valley, aren't you?" Jimmy's mother regarded Agnes Prince. "Her sister Sally is engaged to Howard Gardner. Salina, is Mary still writing Hank?"

Before either girl could answer any of the questions put to them, Agnes Prince said to Jimmy Don, "Put on your coat . . . let's go through the station to escape this wind!"

She took her nephew's hand and headed for the doors, Salina and Scooter close behind, the boy's case thumping Scooter's leg.

Union Station was huge inside. People were everywhere, drinking coffee from paper cups and talking in loud voices. All these people waiting to go places, Salina thought. But where? And if they have to go, why don't they wait till daylight?

It was after five when Agnes Prince swung the automobile left out of the parking lot and turned west onto Broad. Traffic moved rapidly up and down the dark street, headlights flashing. A city bus swerved from the car's path and honked.

"Oh!" Salina said, pressing against the back seat.

Mrs. Prince switched on the car's headlights. "Rush hour." Jimmy Don was between her and his mother.

Scooter gazed out the windows, craning her neck for a good view. "Skyscrapers!" she said. "Oh, boy."

"Not really, Scooter," said Agnes Prince. "They're just two-story buildings. Haven't you girls ever been to Nashville?"

Salina pulled off the woolen hat she had worn and fluffed her unruly hair. "No, Ma'am." Thank goodness, she thought.

Scooter piped up, "But I used to live on Signal Mountain, and that's close to Chattanooga."

Jimmy Don's mother turned slightly in the front seat. "It's a shame you won't have time to see some of the sights."

"Nashville is Tennessee's capital," Mrs. Prince reminded the girls. "The state government buildings are very interesting."

Scooter leaned forward: "What about the Grand Ole Opry?"

"That's behind us. And it's on a side street."

"Oh," Scooter murmured, sitting back in the seat. "Darn."

The lights were on in the houses fronting Broad. Mansions, Salina thought, glimpsing chandeliers, ornate glass doors, and stained glass windows. "What do folks around here do?"

"A lot of things. A city this size needs lawyers—"

"And doctors and nurses!" blurted Jimmy Don.

"Yes, and there's industry and the Cumberland River and Vanderbilt University. Several colleges, in fact." Mrs. Prince turned the automobile onto a narrow street where the houses were close together. Too close, Salina thought. No breathing room.

"Y'all have square dances?" she asked.

"Square—" Jimmy Don's aunt patted the stray hairs at the back of her neck. "Why, I suppose so. A lot of kids your age go ice skating at the public rink, and we have plays."

Something occurred to Salina, and it was so obvious, she could not quite believe she had failed to realize it before. "Mrs. Prince," she said, "is *Gone With the Wind* showing here?"

"It just left! I saw it twice!"

Twice. Envy wormed its way into Salina's veins, followed by disappointment. If she could just *see* the look in Rhett's eyes, *hear* the sound of his voice, she would know his intentions once and for all, but huh-uh.

"Another matinee in another town," Scooter commented matter-of-factly, "and Salina Harris won't be there."

Salina cast the girl a dark look.

"We don't have a skating rink in Pine Valley," Scooter said to Mrs. Prince.

"That's because we don't *need* one," Salina informed Scooter tartly. "In Pine Valley, we wait till Cherokee Pond freezes over, and it's a big, special day."

"What about the highway?" said Mrs. Prince. "Any news?"

"That's right," added Janine. "Do you know its route?"

"No," Salina answered. "My dad mailed a letter Saturday, but he probably won't hear anything. There's this big, huge vacuum that sucks up letters from the Harrises."

Mrs. Prince laughed. "Mother tells me the plan has sparked quite a controversy."

"Some folks are for it," stated the white-haired girl. "It's progress."

"And some *aren't*," Salina added emphatically. "It'll ruin the mountains. There's no sense in changing things that are fine just the way they are."

Mrs. Prince smiled, glancing at her sister-in-law. "Sounds like Mother was right."

At home, Agnes Prince lighted the lamps at either end of the couch. "Girls, the kitchen's down the hall. When you're hungry, just raid the refrigerator. We'll be back home soon. Oh—did Jimmy have lunch?"

"I bought him a sandwich and some milk," Salina answered. "The change is in my pocket—"

"Please, keep it," said Mrs. Prince. "We appreciate your help so much."

"Thank you." Salina glanced at Scooter. She would give Scooter her share of the change later.

While Janine took Jimmy Don to the bathroom,

Mrs. Prince showed the girls to her daughter's upstairs room. "Nancy's spending the night with a college friend."

"This bed's got a tent over it like the ones in the catalogue," Salina observed in wonder.

"A tent? Oh!" exclaimed Mrs. Prince. "That's a canopy, very popular now, and stylish. See, it matches the curtains."

"You make these things?" Scooter asked the woman, inspecting the pink and white bedspread.

"I should say not. We bought everything downtown."

Scooter gingerly touched the bed. "My family quilts. Twelve stitches to the inch. We'd sell you one cheap."

Mrs. Prince stiffened slightly. "You don't like the spread?"

"Oh, no," Scooter protested, "it's not that—it's just that it's thin and the nights are getting colder."

"Don't worry about that. There's a blanket under the bedspread that will keep you toasty warm. Tonight, when I get home from the hospital with Janine and Jimmy Don, I'll show you how to use it. In the meantime, you two make yourselves at home." She started toward the door.

"Mrs. Prince?" Salina called after her.

"Yes?"

"Is there a store downtown that sells stuff for horses?"

The question surprised Mrs. Prince. "I'm not sure. But I can find out . . . why? Do you have a horse?"

"No, but my brother does, and I'd like to get him a Christmas present tomorrow morning. If we have time before catching the train."

"All right. I'll check around." Jimmy Don's aunt shut the bedroom door and was gone.

"Show us how to use a blanket?" Salina grumbled when she was sure Agnes Prince was out of hearing. "How dumb do you suppose she thinks we are?" She ran her hands up and down her ribs. "Everything here's ugly. Just look at the furniture!"

She tapped her finger on the dresser. It was white, trimmed in fake gold paint, and had skinny, curving legs. Why would anyone prefer it to hand-carved furniture like the bedroom suite she and Mary shared? Both their dresser and feather bed had been carved from cherry wood and shipped all the way down the Mississippi River to Tennessee. Old Daddy had been born in the bed, and he had died in it, too, and remembering that sometimes gave Salina a sad and lonely feeling she could not name.

"Sally's Howard would really *hate* this stuff," she said.

Scooter responded predictably: "The Princes just like it, that's all."

"Salina?" a small voice said from behind the

bedroom door. "Scooter?"

The two girls stared at one another, startled to hear Jimmy Don. Salina opened the door.

The boy's thin shoulders sagged. "I'm not going, and you've got to tell my mama and Aunt Agnes."

Mystified, Salina drew Jimmy inside. "What do you mean, you're not going? That's what you came here for!"

Scooter motioned Jimmy to the bed. The pair sat down. "Tell me what's wrong, Jimmy Don."

"Huh-uh," he sniffed.

"Salina," Scooter said, "bring me a damp cloth." Salina did as Scooter asked, and Scooter held the cool wash cloth to Jimmy Don's forehead. "You have to go," she told him softly.

"But I'm scared."

"I know."

"Jimmy Don," Salina said impatiently, "your dad's okay—"

"I *hate* the hospital! Everybody looks scared, and it smells funny. And they have weird stuff stuck in him."

Salina took a step back. "But he's not critical anymore. That was when he was in Sevierville. He's getting well, and he'll be home soon. I promise."

"How did you know I was scared?" Jimmy asked Scooter.

"I just did. But you've got to go to the hospital and visit your dad. You've got to act like an adult."

[125]

She held the cloth against her own flushed cheeks for a moment before folding it and handing it to Salina.

"But I'm not an adult," Jimmy Don protested. "I'm a kid."

"You've got to act like one." Scooter stood and took his hand. "You might be sorry if you don't."

"I might?"

"Cross my heart and hope to die. They're saying your dad's better. He'll probably be okay."

They went down the hall, Jimmy Don gripping Scooter's fingers, Salina staring after them. "My daddy was in the war," she heard Jimmy Don say. "He even got shot fighting the Germans. But that didn't hurt him bad."

Later that evening, when Jimmy, his mother, and his Aunt Agnes arrived home from the hospital, Mrs. Prince came into the bedroom and got on her hands and knees on the floor beside the canopy bed. "Now," she said, "we plug this in here . . . there . . . and set the dial on medium—adjust it later, if you like—and by the time you get undressed and crawl in, the bed will be toasty."

She pulled back the thin bedspread, exposing the pink electric blanket beneath it. Salina stared. "Is something wrong, dear?"

Scooter smiled sweetly. "No, Ma'am."

Agnes Prince hesitated, momentarily unsure. "Well, don't stay up too late. I found a store we can try in the morning, but we'll have to leave a little early." At the bedroom door, she paused once more. "Are you sure you don't want a bedtime snack?"

Salina shook her head. "We ate plenty of potato salad and ham for supper. Chocolate pie, too. Mrs. Prince?"

"Yes?"

"How's Mr. Orange?"

"Fine. He'll be home by Christmas. Nighty-night." She closed the door gently behind herself so as not to disturb Jimmy Don and Janine in the next room.

"That blanket's electric," Salina commented the moment Mrs. Prince's footsteps sounded on the stairway. Crossing the bedroom in a few determined strides, she yanked the cord hard and unplugged it.

Scooter grinned. "I'm glad you did that."

Salina silently removed her blouse and put it with her other clothes on the dresser. "Huh. I thought you were probably *for* electric blankets." In the mirror, she caught a glimpse of herself, a skinny girl dressed in a ribbed camisole and baggy cotton underwear, her wiry red hair puffed out all over her head.

They extinguished the lights and went to bed. Into the darkness Scooter said, "It's real different here, huh?"

"That's the understatement of the year."

Scooter laughed softly. "I liked hearing the radio tonight. There's more to choose from in Nashville than in Pine Valley. Reception's better, too." Slowing a bit, while Salina listened without comment, Scooter mentioned *The Black Stallion Returns.* "When I finish *The Three Musketeers*, I'm going to check it from the bookmobile and read it over again." She yawned and pulled the bedspread to her chin. "I love it. I'd love a horse like that." There followed a silence. "I wonder how Sugar's doing."

"Me, too." And Paul? Salina was certain Paul was babying Sugar-Boy more than ever, since riding him prematurely. She rested her hands beneath her head. "Scooter?"

"Uh-huh?"

"You know when you read *The Count of Monte Cristo* the week before Mayella's Halloween party?"

"Uh-huh?"

"How'd you do it so fast?"

"By reading during lunch at school. I nearly always do that—read, or work on a song. I'm too busy at home, with chores and everything, so I use every spare minute at school I get. Why?"

"I thought you were antisocial."

"Oh . . . G'night."

"Scooter?" Salina said. "You sure did sound grown-up when you comforted Jimmy Don." There was no answer; Scooter was asleep. "Good night," Salina said, but she did not close her eyes. For a long time she lay awake, thinking about people who preferred thin blankets with wires in them to downy handmade quilts.

❧ TWELVE ❧

THE NEXT MORNING, Salina and Scooter left the house early, with Agnes Prince leading the way. There was no rain or snow in the forecast, and yet the sky was gray, the sun hazy.

"What's wrong out here?" Salina asked, her tone worried as they crossed the front porch.

"We're in the Cumberland Valley," said Mrs. Prince. "Nashville's under a pressure system. Sometimes the atmosphere's like this for days."

"I'm real sorry," Salina said, still peering at the dismal sky as they climbed into the car.

Agnes Prince took the girls downtown. First, they went into a department store, where the woman bought some bed sheets. "Store-bought sheets," Scooter remarked to Salina, but Salina only answered, "Huh," because she was busy staring at the store's Christmas decorations, the perfume counter, the shoes . . .

Next stop was a saddlery, whose name Mrs. Prince had gotten from a friend. Salina looked in the display window at the bridles and saddles, thinking of Sugar-Boy. In one corner was a beautiful horse blanket, navy, with a series of red and yellow stripes at either end. When they went inside, the bells attached to the door jingled, announcing their arrival.

The blanket was made of rich wool. Salina touched the ten dollar bill in her jacket, doubting that Paul had ever imagined a blanket this pretty for Sugar.

The price tag said six dollars. More than half her money. Mrs. Prince glanced at her watch. "I'll take it," Salina told the clerk, and watched with a tingle of delight as he wrapped the blanket in brown paper and secured it with heavy string.

Next they went to a bookstore and though at first Salina resisted, finally she relented and bought a copy of *My Friend Flicka*, bringing her personal book collection to five. It looked like everyone but Sugar would have homemade Christmas presents.

"I'd like to have some books of my own someday," Scooter commented as the saleswoman rang up Salina's purchase.

"Why don't you buy one now? You'd have more than enough left for Sally's cologne."

"I'm giving Mom all the money I have left over to take care of Rachel's Santa Claus."

"Hmm," Salina answered, feeling a little embarrassed. She always forgot how poor the Russells actually were. And she was surprised that Scooter concerned herself about Santa Claus.

At Union Station, Agnes Prince hurried the girls aboard the train and before long, to Salina's relief, they were on their way; she couldn't wait to get home. For lunch, using the change Agnes Prince had given them, they bought two apples and colas, and when they were finished with them, they stopped talking to read. The next time Salina looked up, they were approaching Pine Valley. She put down her library book—she was saving *My Friend Flicka*—and gazed silently out the window. Patches of snow glistened on the rolling hills. In the distance, the mountains were white, the pine trees dark, dark green, almost black. Inside the train, Salina shivered. The land looked cold, frozen to the core, and even bigger than she remembered.

John Harris and Sally's Howard were at Pine Valley Station waiting when they arrived that evening. Salina ran onto the platform, dropped her package and the grocery sack full of dirty clothes, and hugged her father's neck.

"Glad to be home?"

"You bet!"

He glanced at the neatly tied bundle at their feet. "What's that?"

"A surprise. How's Sugar?"

"On the mend, I'd say."

Sally's Howard swung Salina around, then Scooter, and the foursome started for the trucks. "How's everybody else?" Salina asked.

"Fine. How was Nashville?"

Before Salina could say a word, Scooter answered, "It was big, like Chattanooga! It was exciting, too." Howard opened the door of his pickup, and Scooter climbed in. "See you in church, Salina."

Brother! Salina silently fussed. That girl just *never* stops! Still, she rolled down the truck window and waved. "Well," she said, once she and her father were on Sand Lick Road heading home. "You miss me?"

"Like a duck misses water. And by the way, you got a letter from New York City while you were gone."

Salina could not believe it. After all this time, the letter had finally come. Yahoo, she silently shouted.

At home, she hurried into the living room. Paul lay asleep in front of the fireplace, one leg hanging off the couch, his muddy work boots tossed onto the floor. Salina raced into the kitchen. In the center of the old oak table lay a white business envelope with her name typed on it.

At the sewing machine sat Mary, Mark beside her, his small hand resting on her shoulder.

Salina snatched the letter and got a dinner knife from the silverware drawer. "What're you doing?" she said to Mary. "Where's Mama?"

John Harris came into the kitchen behind Salina. "She's in our room, putting on her nightgown."

"I'm finishing up my new dress," responded Mary. "I'm wearing it to church on Christmas Eve especially for Hank. Who's the big deal letter from?"

Salina ripped open the envelope. "Margaret Mitchell!"

But the letter was not from Margaret Mitchell. It was from an editor thanking Miss Harris for her interest in Rhett Butler and Scarlett O'Hara. Salina silently scanned the page: *Many people have wondered about the book's ending, but few have written Mrs. Mitchell personally. In public, she never took Scarlett and Rhett's story any further. As to your private inquiry, I'm sorry to say that Mrs. Mitchell died in an accident just a few weeks before you wrote.*

Salina's heart dipped.

A motorist struck her while she was crossing the street in downtown Atlanta.

"Sweetheart?" John Harris said, but Salina had thrown down the letter and was gone, running to the barn.

The building was cold inside, and dark. Sitting on the hard floor with her back to Sugar-Boy's stall, Salina pulled her knees to her chest and tried to think, but she was crying, and there were so many riddles in her brain. An accident! How had such a stupid thing happened? Why hadn't she known? She had written the letter, when all along

—what sense did it make? And her question. It was attached to nothing. Fresh tears started and she sobbed, for herself, and for Margaret Mitchell, and for Rhett Butler and Scarlett O'Hara.

"Salina?"

The barn door opened slightly. Salina wiped her eyes on the sleeve of her jacket. "Yes, Sir?"

"Mind if I come in?"

A moment passed. Salina's mouth tugged down at the corners. "I guess not."

John Harris had a lantern. Sugar-Boy got up and stuck his damp nose over the door of the stall. When Salina stood to pat Sugar, he blinked, his eyes black and moist in the dim light.

"Sugar does look better," Salina said, sniffing and clearing her throat. "Even if I was gone for just a day."

Her daddy ran his hand gently along Sugar-Boy's furry neck. "I'm sorry about the letter."

"You read it?"

"Yes, I did."

"It's not fair! Margaret Mitchell was a famous writer, and she wasn't sick or anything!"

"Try not to let it upset you so much, Salina. Things don't always work out the way you want them to—not for people in books or anyone else." Salina's father put his arm around her. "You never did give me your opinion of Nashville."

A place where people drove at a fast clip through too much noise and traffic; thick traffic carried on a big, wide street called Broad, the same, stupid kind of street where for no reason people were killed trying to get across. A city where kids went ice skating indoors. And yet— Jimmy Don's dad had gotten well at the hospital there, and she had bought Sugar-Boy a beautiful blanket like nothing the Monkey Ward or Sears catalogue advertised. And too, there were stores with a good supply of books for sale.

It was all so confusing, like people for roads and people against them, and how, no matter how hard you fought it, you might start liking someone even if that someone did not always agree with you. And how you could—Salina caught her breath, sharply —how you could suddenly not have much in common with your best friend.

"It's different," she answered at last. "Not quiet, like here. And the air's not sweet. But folks seem to like it okay."

He nodded. "Now, if you're okay, why don't we go on inside? Your mama's anxious to see you."

"*Another* thing about Nashville," she said. They walked toward the house illuminated by the light of the full, bright moon. "If we had gone there just a week or two sooner, I could have seen *Gone With the Wind.*"

On Sunday morning, Salina put the hymnal she had been sharing with Mary back in its slot, fervently hoping Preacher Lyte would keep his announcements brief. That way, in a few minutes she and the rest of the family could climb in the pickup truck and go home: early that morning, her mother had cooked pot roast, potatoes, and carrots for dinner. Maybe that would help her not feel so let down and sorry about the letter from the Macmillan Company.

"As you know," the preacher announced from the podium, "Christmas Tree is coming up. Of course, we'll need a tree to decorate—"

Christmas Tree was the potluck supper held every Christmas Eve in the church basement. This year, it was on Friday. On that night, Brother Lyte's congregation would attend church bringing cakes and cookies and homemade decorations of construction paper and pipe cleaners and leftover pie dough. Every year, Minnie Myrtle Wilson brought peppermint candy canes for the kids. This year, Mark had been chosen to play Joseph in the skit the first-graders would present that night. His best friend, Mandy, was Mary.

Sally's Howard raised his hand. "I'll get the tree." He and Sally were to be married on Christmas Eve, just before the Christmas Tree celebration, and everyone was invited. After the ceremony, the congregation would move from the church to the basement, where the Christmas party always took place.

Paul nudged Salina, gently. "Your *pal* sure didn't waste any time getting away."

For one brief instant, glancing across the church's center aisle, Salina thought she saw

Mayella look over and wave, wearing her white fur coat, her green eyes shining and ready for fun. But Mayella wasn't in church in the flesh; this afternoon, she and Salina wouldn't be getting together. Mayella Crenshaw was gone, the girl waving merrily to Salina, a memory. On Friday, school let out for the Christmas holidays and by Saturday at noon, the Crenshaws were driving to Sevierville, where they would spend the next three weeks with the Johnsons.

Salina drew a shivery breath.

"Brothers and sisters, we have something important to discuss," Brother Lyte said. "On Friday, Allan heard from the Highway Commission." Allan Bagby, the mayor.

"Damn it," Paul muttered beneath his breath. "Damn it, damn it, damn it!"

Salina listened closely to the mayor, unable to believe her ears. The government wanted a highway through the mountains for defense, the mayor said, in case there was another war.

"Another war?" Salina whispered to Paul. "There can't ever be another war—"

And eventually the government wanted to build something Mayor Bagby called an interstate system.

"How about explaining this interstate business in a little more detail?" John Harris stood up and said.

"It's like a giant spider web," answered the mayor. "It'll take years to build and it will create a lot of jobs."

When John Harris suggested they write the

Highway Commission, asking its members to work with the Pine Valley Community, Frank Talley's dad jumped to his feet: "Pay attention to a pack of farmers? They didn't even answer your letter!"

Michael Burmeister raised his hand. "That doesn't mean we should just give up."

"What's this 'we' business, Burmeister?" Homer Joiner demanded heatedly.

That got the veterinarian on his feet. "For your information, Mr. Joiner, my family, way back, lived here. I moved from Louisville to get away from cities and busy streets. No matter what we may think of one another personally, we need to stick together."

Salina squirmed in the pew, watching her father as he sat down, and Anna Harris took his hand. Finally, Homer Joiner said, "Reckon I'm with you, John. Who knows? This time they may even listen."

"All right," Brother Lyte said. "Let's write a letter to Nashville asking those commissioners to consider our needs. And I suggest we go a step further: let's send a man to Nashville representing this congregation. I nominate John Harris."

The vote was unanimous, and early the next morning, Salina's father left for Nashville driving the battered green pickup truck, leaving Paul in charge of things and Salina wondering why it was always her dad who did the thinking and planning and doing.

⤳ THIRTEEN ⤳

ONE WEEK LATER, Howard gathered a gang of kids and set out across Pine Valley in search of a Christmas tree. It was late Sunday afternoon, and sunny, though the wind was freezing.

As they walked through the deep snow into the fir and pine forest, Howard carrying an ax in one hand and pulling the sled with the other, Salina hung back, thinking. Her daddy had been in Nashville for seven days, and they had not heard a word from him. How could they? The telephone lines were icy, so he couldn't phone Miss Minnie and ask her to get a message to them. Salina missed him terribly.

Too, she missed Mayella. "Things don't always work out the way you want them to—not for people in books or anyone else," her daddy had said, and though Salina thought probably he was right and that his comment included friendships, that didn't make the drifting away completely painless. She figured that would mean the friendship hadn't meant much, besides.

So this week, she had walked to Miss Minnie's store, bought Mayella a card with Santa pictured in shiny red stuff on the front, and enclosed in the envelope a set of the fake fingernails Miss Minnie kept on the shelf with the nail polish that had names like Passion Fruit Pink and Delilah Red.

Down into the valley they marched, Salina hanging back and thinking. Hadn't she boasted to Scooter Russell that she would *prove* Rhett returned to Scarlett? "Boy, are you gonna feel dumb," she had said. Salina wished that for once she had kept her big fat mouth shut.

"Let's take the biggest tree ever!" squealed little Rachel, her boots crushing deep into the snow.

That morning in church, Howard had made a general announcement inviting along anyone who wanted to come today. Because of the intense cold, few had taken up the invitation, other than all the Russell kids and most of the Harrises. Mary had not come. Mary was home with the blues, because Hank could not get Christmas leave and would not be around for the holidays as planned; Mary had cried all week, whether creaming the butter and sugar for the Christmas cookies that she, Salina, and Mark were making to give to friends, or chopping apples for the mincemeat pies.

If things around here don't change for the better, Salina thought grumpily, it's not going to be a very joyful Christmas.

"Let's take the biggest tree ever!" Rachel said again.

"The church basement has a low ceiling," Howard reminded the little girl.

"We ought to get a big, fat, round one," Josephine suggested. "Shouldn't we, Jenny?"

Her twin sister giggled, shaking back her long blond hair. "We could call it Minnie Myrtle," she remarked, and glanced at Paul, who paid no attention whatsoever. He and Mark were inspecting trees, branch by branch, shaking off the snow and watching it fall with a soft plop onto the white ground.

Suddenly Mark pointed out a young fir. "There's one!"

"Salina?" Scooter said at Salina's shoulder.

Salina jumped. She had been watching, without much humor, as Frank Talley tripped Abigail and smeared snow in her face. "It's a good thing Frank doesn't try that stuff with me," she said. "Hi," she added to Scooter, returning the other girl's greeting.

"I just wanted to say I'm sorry your dad isn't back," Scooter told Salina quietly. And then she patted Salina's arm in a consoling way.

Salina regarded the other girl in silence, no longer surprised by anything she said and did. She smiled a little. "Thanks. How come you always know how I feel?"

"Like I mentioned once before," the other girl

responded easily, "we have a lot in common."

"Hmmm." Salina watched her breath steam in the freezing air. "There's something I have to tell you." The white-haired girl was silent. "You know I swore I'd prove Rhett Butler returned to Scarlett?"

"Uh-huh."

"It didn't work out."

"I figured it wouldn't." They walked along behind the others. "Well, maybe it is like Miss Williams said and could go either way," Scooter conceded.

"Depending on your attitude," Salina answered. Howard swung the ax in a wide arc. Its blades glinted in the winter sun. "Be careful," she warned.

Howard winked and pulled his red woolen scarf closer around his neck. "Who'll help me hoist this onto the sled?"

Paul tied down the tree with a length of rope he had brought along. Scooter and Mark held the fir in place while Paul worked, his expression intent, his gloved hands deft. From time to time, he glanced at Scooter, and she smiled, her cheeks pink.

"Gonna be a wedding tree," Howard sang as they pulled the sled home. The ceremony was just five days away. He tugged the end of Salina's light blue scarf, and she smiled, feeling settled inside and reasonably content.

On Thursday evening, she stood watching the

trees in the front yard bow to the wind. Gray clouds rolled across the sky, lit by the radiance of a full white moon. The rain came first, hard and furious, then sleet, pelting the panes of glass with ice.

Salina went to the couch and settled before the fire. At the other end of the sofa sat her mother, putting buttons on the shirt she had made John Harris for Christmas. (This morning they had received a telegram from him: he had finally met with the Highway Commission and would be home Christmas Eve. That was tomorrow. He'd probably arrive in the afternoon.) Mark lay on the hearth, turning the pages of an old Sears catalogue in search of paper clothes to cut out for his cardboard dolls. Paul was rattling around in the kitchen, looking for something to eat, though they had just finished supper; and Mary was in the bathroom washing her face. Salina opened her book and immediately looked up, startled at the sound of someone running across the front porch.

Anna hurried to the door and opened it. Scooter Russell stood there, crying. Her coat and hat—her eyelashes—were covered with snow. Mark's mouth fell open. Mary ran from the bathroom, holding a yellow towel. Salina got up from the couch.

Anna Harris quickly drew Scooter inside.

"It's Sally's Howard!" Scooter cried. "He's at the mill, his leg cut. We've got to get him to Hogginsville!"

"The truck's not here—" Salina's mother gestured helplessly. "How bad is he?"

"Terrible," Scooter said in rising panic, "and nobody's around. The Crenshaws are gone and everyone else lives too far away!" She was shaking all over.

Paul strode in from the kitchen, a half-eaten Christmas cookie in one hand. "What's going on?"

"Paul," Scooter said, "Howard was finishing a rocking chair for him and Sally and cut his leg with one of his tools. He's got to see Doc Smith!"

"Howard's still at the mill?"

Scooter nodded. "He didn't show up for supper, so Sally and me went after him and accidentally drove the truck into a ditch. We ran the rest of the way to the mill and found him! He can't walk, and the phones are out because of the storm. Doc Smith better see him, fast—" She drew a sharp breath.

"Don't worry," Paul said after a moment. "I'll go to Hogginsville and get him."

"I'll tell Sally and Howard to hold on." Scooter bolted out the front door, the tassel of her yellow hat bouncing crazily.

Paul brushed past Mary, pulling his heavy jacket from one of the hallway pegs as he went. He was heading for the barn.

"Paul!" Salina called, running outside after him. "What are you doing?" The sleet, mixed with snow, stung her face.

The barn was pitch black inside. Fumbling in

the dark, Paul found the kerosene lamp and the matches. Shadows loomed on the wall. Sugar-Boy stood up in his stall and gazed sleepily at them, blinking against the jarring noise and light.

"You leave Sugar alone!" Salina grabbed Paul's arm.

Paul ignored her, led Sugar from the stall and quickly readied him. Sugar-Boy didn't mind; he was used to the feel of the saddle and bridle. He tossed his head, and with his nose nudged Paul in the side, playfully.

"Paul," Salina persisted, "don't! Or just go as far as the Talley's and let Mr. Talley or Frank take their car! Paul—"

"In that old Chevy, on a night like this? How far do you think they'd get?"

"About as far as you will, riding a half-crippled horse!"

Pushing past her, Paul took Sugar-Boy outside into the swirling snow and mounted him. Surprised by the weight on his back, the horse balked. Then Paul ran his hand along Sugar's neck, calming him, and they rode into the stormy night.

* * *

At a few hours past midnight, Mark shouted, "I hear somebody coming up the drive!" and ran to a window in the living room. "It's Paul, driving Doc Smith's truck!"

They rushed outside, and Paul climbed from behind the wheel. "I need help," he said. He walked around the white pickup, the others close on his heels, and lowered the tailgate. Sugar-Boy lay there, barely breathing. He was foaming at the mouth.

Salina looked away, her throat tight. Sugar looked like he had been ridden to death.

"How's Sally's Howard?" Anna Harris quickly said.

"Fine. He's at home. Doc Smith's there, too. He's waiting for me. Let's get Sugar in the barn."

"Howard's leg is okay?" Mary asked tremulously. She was shaking with cold. She had on fuzzy pink house shoes and a cardigan on over her blue flannel nightgown.

Paul nodded. "It was cut pretty deep, but Sally wrapped it in a blanket and stopped the bleeding. When I got to town and told Doc what had happened, we put Sugar in the back of the truck and headed straight for the mill. We probably should have found a place for Sugar in town, but we were afraid to take the time."

He looked at his mother. "I rode in back with Sugar-Boy while Doc Smith drove Sally and Howard from the mill to the Gardners'. It snowed all over him, Mama. He was freezing."

Anna Harris hugged Paul. "Would you take the truck back?" he said, his voice higher than usual, and thin. "The snow's stopped. Just be careful."

"Of course. A lot of folks are bound to show up, once the news gets out—they'll need extra food. Mary, go get a ham from the barn. Mark, gather some eggs and put them in the truck . . . be careful. And I'll take some sourdough bread—"

Paul turned to Salina. "Let's help my baby inside."

They got Sugar to his feet and down the ramp Paul improvised from several of the wooden planks John Harris had bought that fall to repair the chicken house. The horse wobbled dangerously on his legs; slowly, they guided him into the barn where he sank onto the hay scattered beneath the loft. Salina lingered there while the others gathered their things, watching silently as Paul knelt beside Sugar-Boy and lovingly covered him with his worn old Army blanket. The new one was tucked beneath Salina's feather bed, a Christmas surprise.

She went to the house, retrieved the blanket and took it to the barn, where she silently unwrapped it and handed it, still neatly folded, to Paul. Suddenly, she was embarrassed. "Merry Christmas."

He looked at her, mystified. "What is it?"

"A new blanket for Sugar. I bought it in Nashville." Against her fingers, the fabric of the blanket felt soft and rich and warm.

"Salina," Paul whispered, "that's really nice." He took the navy blanket and spread it gently over Sugar. "It's beautiful, Sis. It'll keep him comfortable." He ran his hand along Sugar's neck, pulling up the blanket a bit, so that it completely covered Sugar's broad back and shoulders.

Salina went to Paul and touched the top of his head; his longish hair felt damp. She wanted to hug him, but she didn't. She walked back outside, and in the early morning light, with Mark in back, holding on to the ham, Anna Harris drove them down Sand Lick Road in Doc Smith's truck, to the Gardners' place.

At dawn, Salina and Mark caught a ride home with Guy Henderson. Anna Harris and Mary had stayed at the Gardners' and weren't coming home till noon. Salina couldn't stand the suspense of knowing about Sugar another minute; the thought of eating the huge breakfast her mother and the other women were cooking sickened her.

"Will Howard have a wooden leg?" Mark asked as the ticket agent maneuvered his truck along the snowy road.

"No," Salina answered. "But there sure won't be a wedding tonight." It was Friday. Christmas Eve.

"We'll still have Christmas Tree, won't we?" Mr. Henderson nodded. "What if Sally and Scooter hadn't gone after Howard?" Mark said then.

Salina gazed out the windows into the cold December dawn. The sun was rising, the sky pink. "He might have bled to death."

Mark put his hand on her knee. "Captain Hook has a wooden leg."

"He does not, Mark, he has a hook. That's why they call him that."

"Oh."

Mr. Henderson grinned.

Salina gazed out the window of the truck, toward the mountain range. The Smokies looked cold and unyielding.

"Will Sugar die?" Mark asked.

"Mark," she said, "just *hush.*"

"How bad is the horse?" asked Mr. Henderson.

"Pretty bad when we left."

"That's a shame; everybody in Pine Valley knows how Paul feels about Sugar." Salina looked at the man but didn't say anything as he brought the truck to a slow stop at the end of their drive.

The house and barn, in full view, were silent and still. Removed from them somehow, like a plastic house and barn scene in a winter paperweight.

"Thanks for the ride." Salina took Mark's hand as he slid off the seat after her.

They walked a few steps, then ran toward the barn, their woolen neck scarves flapping behind them, and found Paul lying alongside Sugar in the hay, one arm around the horse's unmoving neck. Salina caught her breath.

Paul rose anxiously to his feet, brushing twigs from his hair. "Howard?"

"He's okay. He'll be off his leg for a long time, Doc Smith said. He won't be doing any planting this spring."

Sugar heard their voices and tried lifting his head. Relief flooded Salina, then faded as the horse sank back into the hay, weak with the effort of moving. "He's not any better," she said. "He's just laying there getting worse."

"Sugar-Boy," Mark called lightly. He got on his knees and gently ran his hand along Sugar's side. Paul immediately opened his mouth to protest, but instead slid his hands into the pockets of his muddied jeans and kept silent.

Like it doesn't matter anymore, Salina thought bitterly. She wanted to say, I *told* you so! She wanted to smack Paul's pretty face and hurt him. —She wanted to tell him he had done what he had to do, and not to feel so bad.

"Wait a minute," she said. "What about Michael Burmeister?"

"What about him?"

"He's a vet! We can go get him."

Paul planted his hands firmly on his hips. "No way. What's wrong with you?"

"This is Sugar-Boy we're talking about!"

Mark looked from Salina to Paul. "I think it's a good idea."

"No lousy Kraut's touching my horse."

Salina stamped her foot. "That is so *stupid*, Paul Harris! He's not even really from Germany. And so what if he was?"

"He's *not* part of the valley. He's an outlander, which you've said a million times yourself! You sure have changed your tune—"

Salina gritted her teeth and heard herself yell, "WHO CARES?!" Then she sprinted from the barn and down the drive, following the tire tracks Mr. Henderson's truck had pressed into the snow.

❧ FOURTEEN ❧

SHE RAN THREE MILES down the snowy, glisten-ing road, her nose and throat aching with cold, before Willard Cates stopped and drove her the rest of the way to town. Michael Burmeister answered Mrs. Imy's doorbell, wearing striped pajamas and a navy robe.

"You've got to come with me," Salina said in a rush. "Our horse is bad off—"

"Wait in the truck. I'll get my bag."

On the road, still shivering, Salina related Sugar-Boy's history and told the veterinarian about Paul's ride to help Sally's Howard.

"And Sugar wasn't ridden much before last night?" He had pulled on trousers and had a coat on over his pajama top.

"Paul's been putting weight on him a little at a time. He finally rode him a few weeks ago, and Sugar took it hard. Paul didn't mean to hurt him. He just wanted to ride him, I guess. Paul's really good with Sugar. I've been helping some."

"I see. How was Sugar-Boy when you left them a while ago?"

"Terrible. He can't stand up."

"Exhaustion. Our main concern is pneumonia. I wish he was on his feet, Salina. Once a horse is down—" He left the statement unfinished.

As they entered the barn, Paul took a protective stance beside Sugar-Boy, who was resting on his breastbone in the scattered hay. Mark had gone into the house.

The veterinarian assessed Paul's negative attitude in an instant, brushed past him, and was immediately on his knees beside Sugar. "His temperature is elevated," he commented softly. "And his pulse is hard."

A heavy, yellowish discharge slowly drained from Sugar's nostrils.

Burmeister ran his hands beneath the two blankets and gently examined Sugar's side and neck. "You've kept him warm. That's good. Has he been eating?" Silence engulfed the barn. "I am not the enemy," Burmeister added with an edge to his voice.

Still, there was silence.

"He doesn't want much," Paul answered finally. "Especially not grain. But he's craving water, so I've been giving him some a little at a time."

"How've you managed that?"

He indicated the cloth and bucket of water on the floor. "By letting him suck."

"I told you Paul was good with him," Salina said. "But why's Sugar laying like that?" Sugar's position in the hay looked awkward and uncomfortable.

The veterinarian straightened the blankets. "So he can breathe. He has pneumonia. His lungs are infected. The first thing I'm going to do is give him a shot of penicillin and supplement his water with vitamins."

"You're giving him a shot?" Salina said. "Like you would a person?"

"He's not a pet like Mrs. Imy's dog," Paul said curtly.

"You love him, don't you?" Burmeister didn't expect an answer; he took the necessary items from his bag and deftly injected Sugar-Boy in the rump.

"Now," he said softly, "we wait."

"For what?" Salina asked, her voice rising.

Burmeister put away his things. "Tomorrow morning, I'd say." He smiled slightly. "Christmas. Paul's taken excellent care of Sugar; that's worth a lot. And penicillin has been known to work miracles." He glanced at Paul. "You did a noble thing last night." Paul held the older man's gaze, then looked away, his hands on his hips, and said nothing.

Salina and the veterinarian walked outside, their boots crunching on the snow and ice. In a nearby tree, a bird chirped joyously. And the sun shone high overhead, as if the world had not suddenly tilted.

At the pump in the barnyard, the veterinarian rinsed his hands in icy water, shook them briskly, and stuck them into the pockets of his coat.

Salina said quietly, "Sugar saved Howard's life."

"I know."

"My dad will pay you." She walked with him to the pickup truck. "He should be back home any time now."

Burmeister climbed into the truck and put his bag on the seat. "Inside just now I said Paul did a noble thing. Given the way some people around here feel about me, so did you. Thanks for deciding to come after me this morning."

Salina shielded her eyes against the sun's glare on the snow and ice. "There was no deciding to it, Doc. Something just rose up inside me and shouted, 'Go on!'"

"Doc?" The young vet laughed as he started the truck's engine.

Salina smiled briefly with him. "Doctor Burmeister," she said, "sometimes you remind me of Ashley Wilkes."

"I accept the compliment," he said, and put the truck in gear. "Tell Paul I'll be back this afternoon to check on things. And I'll see you tonight, at Christmas Tree."

Salina watched the truck pull carefully down the slick drive, then she straightened her shoulders and headed back toward the barn, Sugar-Boy, and her noble brother, Paul.

That evening countless stars and a pale round moon illuminated the snowbound countryside. The night air whipping around the bed of the pickup froze Salina's ears; reaching up, she pulled the rim of her hat closer around her face and tucked in the wisps of red hair escaping around the edges.

Wish Daddy could afford a car, she reflected gloomily. Then we wouldn't have to ride everywhere in this old truck.

For a while that afternoon, Salina had thought they might not go to Christmas Tree. Or anyway, not Paul, whose heart was not in it. Exhausted from the previous night's events and her early morning trip to town for Michael Burmeister, she had fallen asleep across the feather bed with Mary and had slept soundly till the familiar rattle of their father's truck woke them; when they reached John Harris, Paul, who had come quickly from the barn, was telling him about Sally's Howard and Sugar-Boy.

In the last few hours, nothing had changed: Sugar was still listless and unwilling to eat. "But Burmeister says he'll be okay in the morning," Paul was saying.

Salina pursed her lips. Paul's statement was not exactly true. When Michael Burmeister returned earlier in the afternoon to double-check on Sugar, he had expressed hope, but that was all.

John Harris returned their hugs warmly and mussed Mark's hair. "Well, thank God Howard's okay." He glanced toward the barn, his expression deeply concerned. "Aren't you all freezing?" In their haste to greet him, they had ignored their coats and gloves.

"No," Salina smiled, thankful he was home and safe.

"John?" Anna slipped into his waiting arms and they embraced, his plaid coat engulfing her. She gazed up at him questioningly: "What about the highway? Did they tell you the route?"

He shrugged his broad shoulders lightly. "Given the arguing the commissioners do in their meetings, it'll be a while longer before they reach a decision."

She stared at him, nonplussed. "You spent all this time in Nashville and didn't—"

"You know how those people are. I was just lucky I finally got to see them. I didn't exactly have an appointment."

She gazed at him an extra moment, but made no further comment, and after a bit, with Mary and Mark flanking her, she returned to the house, shivering with cold.

"You went after Burmeister?" John Harris asked Salina.

"Yes, Sir." In the light of recent events, the road issue—its route—seemed to her very distant.

As they headed toward the barn alongside Paul, John Harris slipped his hand into hers, his cowhide glove thick and textured. "Good," he commented simply.

Paul didn't say a word.

Later, in the kitchen, while John Harris sipped a cup of strong hot coffee, they discussed the Christmas Eve celebration.

Paul leaned against the Frigidaire and folded his arms decisively over his chest. "I'm staying here with Sugar."

Salina's place at the kitchen table gave her a clear view of the living room. Earlier, coming inside the house with Paul and her father, she had plugged in the tiny colored bulbs strung around the Christmas tree; for the first time since they had decorated it, the fat green fir twinkled with light. And Mary had built a fire in the fireplace, the room was warm and cheerful: a holiday house at last.

"I'll stay with you," she said.

"People are counting on us," Anna Harris remarked.

Mary agreed, indicating the mincemeat pies in a row on the counter. "They'll go to ruin if they aren't eaten soon."

"Yeah," Mark said. The pumpkin pies he had made were on the counter with the others.

Too, there were the gifts to consider. Salina had several to give, to her friends Abigail and Jolene . . . and one to Scooter Russell . . . and some to open, including the brown-wrapped, cylindrical-shaped oddity that had arrived from Mayella Crenshaw in Thursday's mail.

"I'm not forcing anyone to do anything," John Harris said, and put his coffee cup on the stove.

"But it is Christmas Eve and I'd like to go or stay as a family. I don't mean to lay this on you, Paul." He smiled gently. "I'm sure we could handle those pies ourselves."

"I'd rather not go," Paul said.

"You need a good supper," Anna said. "You could eat, then come home—someone's bound to leave early tonight. You wouldn't have any trouble getting a ride."

Mark, who had perched beside Paul on the counter, broke in. "Anyway, how can they have the Christmas play without Joseph?"

And that was how it was decided that they all would go to Christmas Tree that night.

❧ FIFTEEN ❧

IN ONE CORNER of the church basement stood the fir taken from deep in the snowy forest. Scooter and Jimmy Don were admiring the presents scattered beneath it, the boy dressed in regular boy's clothes, his father and mother nearby, Janine's hands on the back of her husband's wheelchair. Tommy Orange had been home for almost two weeks.

Scooter and Jimmy Don found Salina almost at once. "Merry Christmas!" said Scooter.

Jimmy Don tugged Salina's sleeve: "Where's Mark?"

"With Mom and Mandy. They're upstairs, getting ready for the play."

The boy raced across the room and up the stairs, shouting, "Yeow!"

"Merry Christmas," Salina said. "How's Howard feeling tonight?"

"His leg hurts like crazy, even with Doc Smith's

pain medicine. Know what, though? He and Sally are getting married in March. Mama gave them their wedding quilt this afternoon. I'm saving Sally's Evening in Paris for in the morning—but how's Sugar?"

"He's got pneumonia. Dr. Burmeister gave him a shot of penicillin. That can work a miracle, he said."

Scooter nodded quietly. "Want some boiled custard?"

They went to the refreshment table, where Rebecca Williams served them each a cup of cold liquid custard from the church's heavy glass punch bowl. Like eggnog, boiled custard was sweet and creamy, but it was cooked before you drank it.

"I hear Dr. Burmeister came to your house in his pajamas this morning." Miss Williams laughed, glancing, at the same time, at the veterinarian, who was across the room, talking with Mary.

"And wearing his coat on over 'em!" bellowed Minnie Myrtle Wilson as she emerged from the crowd and handed each girl a peppermint candy cane. "Sure was good of him to rush out like that."

Salina accepted the striped cane with pleasure, a holdover from when she was a kid. "Thanks," she said to the woman's wide, retreating back. "Thanks a whole lot, Miss Minnie." To Scooter, she added, "Miss Minnie's candy canes are something you can still depend on."

Miss Williams said, "Sally's at the Gardners' tonight?"

Salina didn't answer; Paul had joined Mary and Michael Burmeister. She regarded them with interest, surprised to see her brother with the vet.

"Yes, Ma'am," Scooter said and took a drink of the sweet custard.

"She's lovely, your sister."

Scooter grinned, unaware of the boiled custard mustache beneath her nose. "Yes, Ma'am."

"So beautiful and serene."

Salina put down her cup. "What's 'serene,' Miss Williams?"

"It means being calm, Salina. And it comes from being at peace with yourself."

"I guess it comes naturally to Sally."

"No," her teacher said thoughtfully. "It doesn't come naturally to anyone."

Salina could not think of an answer.

Paul came over then. "Hello," he said quietly to the girls, and nodded to Miss Williams. The young woman offered him a Christmas cookie, which he politely refused, and she served Maudie Cates.

"Merry Christmas," Scooter said.

"Merry Christmas, Scooter. I'm leaving after the program, Salina. That's when the Cates are heading home."

"I'll tell Mom and Dad."

"I was just talking to Doctor Burmeister."

"I noticed."

"He asked me to make rounds with him in a few days. I told him I might."

"You sure have changed your tune," she said,

echoing the words he had used that morning.

"Maybe. The fact is, I might try being a vet myself. Doc Burmeister says there are a lot of good schools around." Paul's voice brightened. "You should have seen him, Scooter. He came busting in this morning and took over like nothing I've ever seen—didn't even take time to completely change clothes."

Scooter rocked back on her heels. "I heard."

Brother Lyte called from near the Christmas tree, "May I please have your attention? I thought John Harris might have a word for us. Got back from Nashville this afternoon. John?"

"I'd best go find Mama," said Scooter.

"Okay."

"Oh," Scooter added, "I told her I'm spending the night with you Monday. I'll come over early." As she turned away, she glanced over her shoulder and grinned, certain of Salina's acceptance, and in that casual glance Salina saw the truth: the undercurrent of their friendship was stronger than their differences.

"Okay," she said, smiling back. "See you later."

"What's the word?" Homer Joiner called to her daddy.

"Yes," said another farmer. "How'd it go?"

"The commission plans to work with us," John Harris answered. With that, he strode to the refreshment table, where Michael Burmeister was serving custard with Miss Williams.

"But what exactly did they say?" James Talley insisted.

"They're not out to steal anybody's farmland. But we can discuss the road later, James. I believe a meeting's been set for Monday night."

"That's right," agreed the mayor. "Six o'clock, upstairs." Several of the men nodded.

"Your mother said for you to be sure and try Miss Minnie's pecan pie," John Harris said to Salina. He wrinkled his nose affectionately.

"If it's as good as it was Labor Day, Mary's probably off in a corner eating it all."

Turning away, he accepted the custard Michael Burmeister offered. "Tonight I could use something a bit stronger than this," he commented to the vet in a soft voice.

Salina pricked up her ears; her daddy thought she had moved on to the pecan pie.

"How bad is it?" the younger man said.

"They're taking land, all right. They'll negotiate and pay top price, but still—" John Harris massaged his eyebrows with his thumb and forefinger. "There'll be trouble. I can't forget the sight of those surveyors working so close to my land. I just didn't want to spoil the holidays for everyone."

Salina backed off, into Paul, who was talking with Sue-Sue Bagby, the mayor's pretty daughter, and Freddie Marshall. Two years older than Paul and Sue-Sue, Freddie was home on leave from the Air Force. He was wearing his blue wool uniform.

Paul frowned darkly. "Another war? We just got through fighting one!"

"I didn't say there was going to be another *world* war," Freddie protested. "Just might come a *little* one. Just enough to keep us hopping!"

Salina mashed her hair down around her head. "What are you talking about?"

"Man talk," said the young soldier, his eyes shining.

"Freddie says there's trouble brewing in Korea," explained Paul. "Could boil over soon. That may be why Hank couldn't get home for Christmas."

"If it does," Freddie said, regarding Paul, "you can bet Uncle Sam'll put *your* name on his list!"

Sue-Sue smiled sweetly up at Paul, and Salina stared at him. "What about going off to school?" she said. "What about being a vet?"

"What's wrong with you?" he said crossly.

"Nothing," she whispered.

The Christmas program was short. Mark and Mandy played Joseph and Mary; afterward, everyone opened presents.

"Salina," said Scooter, coming over with a package. "This is from me to you."

A patchwork apron. Salina smiled, though she didn't have any intention of becoming a cook.

"Thanks," she said. "I love it." She tied the apron around the waist of her corduroy jeans and performed a little dance.

Scooter beamed with anticipation as she opened

the package Salina handed her. "Salina," she gasped, clasping Salina's copy of *My Friend Flicka* to her chest. "Do you really want me to have this?"

"Sure," Salina said. "I already read it."

"Thanks." Scooter happily showed the book around. "Thanks a lot!"

"Howard sent Paul something," Brother Lyte announced, drawing the crowd's attention.

Wrapped in the tissue paper Paul carefully unfolded lay one of Howard's small carvings. This one was of a cantering horse, head held high, tail flying . . . exactly like Sugar-Boy.

Paul gazed intently at the small wooden figure. "Tell Howard I said thanks," he told Scooter. He pressed the carving against his cheek and slipped it into the pocket of his shirt before going to get his jacket.

"Salina," Brother Lyte said into the silence, "why don't we see what Mayella sent you?"

Inside the cardboard tube was a poster. Salina unrolled it carefully, thinking peevishly, What the heck? Why would Mayella send me something so dumb? She sucked in her breath, caught completely by surprise. The poster was the movie advertisement for *Gone With the Wind.* On it, Rhett embraced Scarlett passionately, while Atlanta burned orange in the background. Rhett's face was in profile. Salina could not see his eyes.

"It's nice, Salina," Scooter said quietly, and Salina nodded.

After a moment, when she thought no one would notice, she slipped outside to sit in the pickup truck. The Cates' automobile was gone; Paul was on his way home to Sugar-Boy. Her daddy came up behind Salina. "Here," he said, and opening the truck door, handed in Salina's jacket. "Want me to go away?"

"No." She watched through the windshield as he walked around the front of the truck. He climbed behind the wheel, and for a time, they sat in silence.

"Know what you're getting for Christmas?"

"A nightgown, I hope. Mine's too short."

"You're getting taller, sweetheart. Before you know it, the boys will be hanging around, asking for walks down by Abrams Creek."

She gave him an owlish look. "Any old boy comes hanging around me and I'll pop him a good one."

He grinned. "I don't doubt that for a minute, Salina."

"Brrr," she whispered after a moment. The forest was cold and dark, the snowbound countryside pale in the watery moonlight.

"Cold?"

"Uh-huh."

"Spring will be here before you know it, warming things up."

"Just like clockwork," Salina answered, quoting Paul.

"Hank'll be home for Easter, Mary said. And you know what?"

"What?"

"Unless I'm mistaken, when good weather comes around again, Paul'll be at the Russells, helping out."

Salina glanced at her father: did he mean because of Scooter, as well as wanting to help Sally's Howard? She remembered Sue-Sue Bagby standing close to Paul, smiling at him like sugar. "I'd be afraid to hazard a guess. A lot sure has happened lately." Sometimes she wished she could just wake up on the first day of school and start all over again.

"A lot's always happening, Salina. Things are always changing and flowing together. People, too. You. Me. Everybody. It would be a dull old world, otherwise."

She looked at him, her head cocked. "I hadn't thought of that. But, Daddy. What if the worst happens and the surveyors say that highway's coming smack through our house?"

He gazed thoughtfully at her. "I guess I'll just have to get my shotgun and run them off the way Paul tried to do."

He grinned at the startled expression on her face. "I don't know, Salina. We'll cross that bridge when we get to it. In the meantime, there's something I want to ask you."

"What?"

"Did you know Old Daddy bought our farm

with the money he got from selling his land to make way for the park?"

"No, Sir," she said in surprise.

"Not just my father. A lot of people were able to buy better land, build bigger houses, and send their kids to better schools. And do you know what else?"

She shook her head.

"In those days, there were loggers in the mountains," he said. They wanted every tree in sight. They went to court to stop the park from coming in. Thank God, they lost. If it weren't for the park, the forests would have been razed. Turning the loggers out saved the woodlands."

Salina gazed out the truck windows. In the distance, wisps of fog clung to the mountains. Dark, impressive mountains. And suddenly, it came to her that even the mountains had given up a part of themselves to survive and grow. Things changed. There were surprises. In the end, that was about all you could say.

". . . But Dad?"

"Yes?"

". . . What do you *really* think about Sugar-Boy?"

"I talked with Burmeister a while ago. This afternoon he couldn't make any promises. Doctors never should. But he thinks Sugar will recover. Honestly."

Tears of relief stung Salina's eyes. "I was real scared," she whispered.

"Me, too," her daddy said.

She looked out the truck window, her gaze drawn to the frozen countryside. One fine day, when the earth warmed and the laurel bloomed on the mountains, down in Pine Valley she and Paul would ride Sugar the way they had planned. Over the meadows and past the tulips opening their scarlet buds to the sun they'd go, Sugar's silky mane streaming in the wind.

And Mark, too.

"Whooo?" an owl called from the depths of the forest, and something stirred in the night.

"Don't you think we ought to go inside now?" Salina's father said. "Folks will be worried about us out here in the cold."

They got out of the truck and started for the church. The sounds coming from the basement were soft and muffled and ragged, like the sounds of a radio turned down low. Salina and her daddy's voices were whispers drifting through the pines and snowy forest.

Salina fluffed her hair with her fingers. "Daddy?"

"Yes?"

"You got a handkerchief?"

"Don't I always?"

"Did you ever read *Peter Pan*?" she asked.

"No," he said. "What happens?"

Salina blew her nose and sniffed. "Wendy grows up and forgets how to fly. Isn't that sad?"

"Yes," he answered. "It is."

"Daddy?"

"Yes, Ma'am?"

"This handkerchief's not exquisite like the lacy ones Scooter told me Howard bought for Sally, but I reckon it'll do. Thanks."

"Anytime, Salina." He accepted the used hanky with a smile. "By the way, what are you going to do with the poster Mayella sent you?"

She glanced up at him, her brown eyes bright and defiant: "Put it on my bedroom wall so Scarlett and Rhett'll be the first thing I see every morning when I wake up."

He laughed outright. "Good for you, Salina."

She took a deep breath of the frosty night air and grinned at him: "Merry Christmas, Dad."

"Merry Christmas, Salina," he said. "Now, let's go inside and celebrate."